Zeus

WATER RESCUE

DOGS WITH A PURPOSE

Also by W. Bruce Cameron

Bailey's Story

Bella's Story

Cooper's Story

Ellie's Story

Lacey's Story

Lily's Story

Max's Story

Molly's Story

Shelby's Story

Toby's Story

Lily to the Rescue

Lily to the Rescue: Two Little Piggies

Lily to the Rescue: The Not-So-Stinky Skunk

Lily to the Rescue: Dog Dog Goose

Lily to the Rescue: Lost Little Leopard

Lily to the Rescue: The Misfit Donkey

Lily to the Rescue: Foxes in a Fix

Lily to the Rescue: The Three Bears

DOGS WITH
A PURPOSE

Zeus
WATER RESCUE

W. Bruce Cameron

ILLUSTRATIONS BY
Richard Cowdrey

STARSCAPE

TOR PUBLISHING GROUP
NEW YORK

ZEUS: WATER RESCUE

Copyright © 2023 by W. Bruce Cameron

Reader's guide copyright © [TK]

All rights reserved.

A Starscape Book
Published by Tor Publishing Group
120 Broadway
New York, NY 10271

www.tor-forge.com

The Library of Congress Cataloging-in-Publication Data is available upon request.

ISBN 978-1-250-81556-9 (hardcover)
ISBN 978-1-250-81557-6 (ebook)

Our books may be purchased in bulk for promotional, educational, or business use.
Please contact your local bookseller or the Macmillan Corporate and Premium
Sales Department at 1-800-221-7945, extension 5442, or by email at
MacmillanSpecialMarkets@macmillan.com.

First Edition: 2023

Printed in the United States of America

0 9 8 7 6 5 4 3 2 1

For the newest member of Clan Cameron—Welcome, Arlo!

Zeus

WATER RESCUE

DOGS WITH A PURPOSE

One

Something was happening to my puppy family.

Up until now, my world was made up of my littermates and a man named Roger. (Roger was the one who'd come up with the brilliant idea to feed us soft food.) There was also my mother dog and the yard we lived in. We were all given names (I was Zeus) and this was life—wonderful, wonderful life.

But one day two women and a child came and played with my sister Lady, and when they left, Lady went with them. Then my brother Henry departed with a full human tribe—too many children to count! Next it was Snoopy who vanished. And very much to my surprise, not long after that, my mother left too.

My mother and my littermates, it occurred to me, were all getting *families*. The thought made me swoon. Roger didn't spend much time with us. I enjoyed loping around in the sun and the grass with other dogs to keep me company, but it would be even better to have a family all my own—a bunch of people dedicated to *me*.

Except this didn't happen. No families came to take my brother Troy or me. Troy and I regarded each other warily. For some reason, we were just not good enough to have our own families. Did it have something to do with the fact that we were the two biggest of the bunch? Did people like smaller puppies better? I worried about it a lot as I lay in the grass and chewed sticks or Troy's ear or now and then my own front paws, just to see what they tasted like.

Why wasn't Troy good enough to get a family? Why wasn't I?

A long time passed, and then one day the gate opened. Troy and I went berserk, because a new family walked in, with a woman and a man and many human children. "Troy, Zeus, this is the ʻŌpūnui family," Roger announced to us.

The children separated me from my brother, giving us each undivided attention. So many feet and ankles to sniff. So many fingers to lick. So many hands stroking me. *Yes*, this is what I wanted.

I had finally met my family.

"You said these puppies were born on a farm?" the woman asked, reaching down for Troy. I watched jealously as he squirmed in her arms.

"That's right," Roger told her. "Pregnant female just showed up at the farm one day, no microchip, no collar."

"These are such beautiful chocolate Labradors. I don't know how you do it." The woman gave Roger a sad smile. "I'd want to keep all of them for myself."

"Animal rescue is hard," Roger admitted. "We don't let ourselves fall in love. Finding them new homes is more important."

"So how does this work?" the adult man asked. He stroked Troy's head, but I was not too jealous because a boy and a girl were focusing warm, happy attention on me, rubbing my soft, round belly until I groaned with happiness.

Roger nodded. "I told you on the phone about Marco Ricci. He's a paramedic and a member of the Oahu Search and Rescue team. He'll be out in a few days to decide which dog he wants—I reserved the two smartest ones for him. Then, if you want, you can have the other one."

"Oh, we want, we definitely *want*," the woman assured Roger.

"He sounds like an interesting guy," the man observed.

"Marco? Oh yes, that's the perfect word, *interesting*," Roger replied with a chuckle. "Extremely organized and strategic. If he says he'll be here at 10:35, that's when he'll arrive. But the guy came back from a visit to family in Italy with the idea of training dogs in water rescue, and now they say he's just about the best in the world."

"I don't know that we're good at dog training, but

we'll certainly give Troy or Zeus a lot of love!" the man said with a smile.

The man and woman took a turn petting me next, while some of the children played Tug-on-a-Stick with Troy. Everything seemed to be going just as it should. So Troy and I were stunned when the family left without taking either of us. We had been so good!

Many more days passed without families. I felt pretty confident that Troy was the problem.

One morning we were sleeping deeply when I had a sense that someone new had arrived. Both Troy and I blearily opened our eyes to find a man kneeling right there, smiling down at us. I sniffed his hands, finding a rich, earthy odor and strong traces of dog. The man's eyes and hair were dark like Roger's, but his arms and hands were lighter.

Roger watched approvingly as Troy and I found our energy and leaped up at the new man's face, trying to lick him. "I already have a family lined up for whichever one you don't pick, Marco. That one's Troy, and that one's Zeus," Roger told him. I heard my name, but I was focused on this man, chewing his hands with affection so that he would understand that I, and not Troy, should be his dog.

I was pretty surprised when he scooped us both up and stood. Troy and I stared at each other, amazed to be so high off the ground.

"Thanks for holding them for so long," the new man

said cheerfully. "I know it's easier to adopt out younger puppies, but there's really no way to test them before they're three months."

Roger shrugged, "You do enough for our rescue, Marco. And like I said, I've already got a family for the one you decide isn't good enough."

"Oh," the man corrected, "I'm sure they're both good. But to work in water rescue you need to be *fearless*. By the end of the day, I'll know if one of these can make it through the program."

I had never been beyond the gate of our yard, so when the man stepped through it, my nose was in the air, drinking in new smells. The man smiled down at us. "Ready for a ride in the Jeep?"

He put us in a crate in the back of a car and closed the door. Next to us was another crate, with another dog in it! He was male and huge, with a white face spotted with what looked like mud splatters. Troy and I climbed on top of each other to get a better look. "That's Bear," the man told us before he moved around to sit in the front of the car.

"All right, little guys, let's go find out which one of you will be the next water rescue dog!" he called back to us.

Soon we felt ourselves *moving*. Troy splayed his legs out nervously. I lifted my nose to the amazing assortment of scents that were streaking by, a jumble of birds and flowers and other living things, most obviously the big dog next to us. A deep rumble vibrated up through the floor.

Was this where our siblings had gone when they were carried out of the gate by their new people?

After a while, the rumble ended and we stopped moving. Troy fell down. Sharp, clean, nearly overwhelming fragrances flowed into my nose. The man took us out of the crate and set us down on warm pavement.

"What've you got here, Marco?" a delighted woman asked. This was when I decided that Marco was the name of the man who'd brought us here, the way Roger was Roger and I was Zeus and Troy was Troy.

The woman was shorter than Marco and carried the same strong scents as the air—it blotted out everything else, this fiercely clean odor.

"Aloha, Jessica. This is Troy and Zeus."

"And this is the famous Bear," she said delightedly, as the big dog dropped down next to us. Troy and I instantly nosed him, climbing on him, loving him. He regarded us with a dour expression while we tried to bite his jowls. "He's so big!"

"Bear's face is English Setter, but his body's all Newfoundland, like his mother."

"He's beautiful! Okay, you've got the whole day. The water park's closed to the public for spring inspection," the woman told Marco.

"That's more time than I need. All I'm looking for today is a sense of how they react to scary things, like waterslides and wave pools. A rescue dog needs to think of water like air—something to move through."

"Have fun," the woman said with a smile.

"Okay, dogs. Dogs!" We heard the sharp note in Marco's voice and looked up in amazement. For some reason, he ran away from us! Didn't he like us?

But the big dog followed Marco, so we followed the big dog. Now I understood—we were playing a chase game! We ran through some sort of gate and across a stretch of concrete that was slick and hard under my paws. I realized very quickly that Troy was faster than I, which was frustrating. Whatever we were doing, I wanted Marco to love me the most for doing it.

Marco reached the sloping edge of a pool of clear, glassy water. This was where the sharp smells came from—the water! It didn't smell anything like the water in my bowl back in the yard.

Marco didn't stop. He just kept running, right into that strange-smelling water. It started out very shallow and quickly got deeper, up over his ankle, then as deep as his knees.

Bear didn't hesitate, so Troy and I didn't either, plunging after him, galloping, then lunging, and then finally swimming to catch up with Marco. He waded ahead of us and then turned and smiled. "Look at you! You're such good dogs!"

Troy and I reached Marco and didn't know what to do next. I tried to climb up Marco's legs, but that didn't work. The water splashed into my nose and I sneezed and paddled as hard as I could.

"Come on, Zeus! Come, Troy! Come, Bear!" Marco turned and waded energetically back to shore. "Let's go to the river!"

The big dog, I decided, was called Bear.

We followed Marco across more pavement and reached a place where the pavement ended. More of the clear, pungent water flowed past, moving quickly.

Marco and Bear didn't even stop. They just kept moving, jumping into the air and then dropping through the water's surface.

I was running so fast that I couldn't stop even if I'd wanted to. In a moment, I was over the edge, and then I was falling. I sank in bubbles and bobbed up, blinking, totally confused.

Bear was swimming in circles around Marco, so I followed. Swimming felt a little like running, except it was harder work to push my legs through the water than to gallop along the ground.

Marco stood and water parted around him. When I went toward him, the paddling was easy. But if I tried to head away from him, the water pushed at me, hard. I had to struggle to keep moving.

"Zeus! Oh, that was good. Look at you, brave puppy!" He glanced up. "Come on, Troy!"

Troy was still on the pavement, some distance above us, wagging anxiously. He did *not* want to make the leap. But I could tell he wanted some of the approval Marco was showing me. Perhaps my brother had figured out the same thing I had, that making Marco happy would mean having a family.

So, with a final glance at me, Troy flung himself off the perch, falling into the water to be with us. He went under and came up sputtering. "Good dog. Good dog," Marco told him. I didn't know what this meant, but I heard the approval. Troy and I had figured out how to please Marco.

Marco boosted us out of the water and then we did the same trick over and over, moving along the stream. Each time, the edge we jumped from was higher and the water below us was deeper. Troy's hesitation had vanished, making us equals, as far as I could tell. That was too bad. I didn't mind if Marco liked Troy, but I wanted him to like me more.

"Such good dogs," Marco praised both of us.

I liked hearing that, whatever it meant. Marco's voice was happy, and I liked making him happy.

"All right, let's do the wave pool."

By this time I'd decided that whatever was going on, I should just mimic the big dog. When Bear swam out after Marco into a wide, flat pond, I followed. Swimming was getting easier, and I was starting to understand how to keep my nose high enough that the water would stay out of it.

I was astounded to be tossed high when the water suddenly swelled and crashed. Troy decided he'd had enough and went for shore, but I hung with Bear and Marco.

"You're fine. See, it's just a wave. You're fine," Marco told me.

We swam in the middle of the pool as one mound of water after another came at us. The mounds swept me up high and then slammed down on my head, dunking me under. It was very strange and confusing, but I learned that I'd bob up to the surface every time, so it wasn't too bad. And Marco was happy.

Finally, we joined Troy at the edge of the unstable pool. I could tell my brother was as tired as I was, even though all he'd done was run around and yap, anxiously watching us get tumbled by water.

"Just one more thing," Marco promised. We followed on his heels, no longer full of berserk energy but just keeping pace as he trotted over to a set of stairs.

He reached down and gathered up Troy. I watched in distress as Marco climbed up with my brother under his arm. Bear mounted the steps under his own power.

I was alone! Would a yip be appropriate? I put a paw on the first step and looked up, wagging in confusion. How was I supposed to get up there? My brother peered at me smugly from under Marco's arm, clearly assuming he was the one chosen.

But Marco understood what was wrong. I loved Marco! He came back and carried me up next to Troy, and we were again equals. We were on a small platform high above a bright, glistening pool. There was barely room for all us.

Marco sat down. "Okay, I promise you, this will never happen in real life. Who wants to go first?" He scooted himself forward until his legs were dangling over the edge of the platform, his feet pointed down a long, wet ramp. "Ready for the slide? You ready, Troy? Zeus, you want to do the slide?"

I thought of this new place as Slide.

Then, to my utter shock, Marco pushed himself off with his hands and shot down the ramp. He was gone! He fell into the pool with a massive splash, and I whined with worry. But a moment later he stood up in the water, clapping his hands. "Bear!"

The big dog leaped forward and plummeted down, into the pool. I stared in disbelief, utterly astounded that a dog could do something like this!

"Okay, Zeus. Okay, Troy. Come!"

I was beginning to understand that word, *Come*. Marco seemed to use it when he wanted us all to be together. But why was he saying it *now*? The slide was between us, keeping us apart!

I gazed down the steep ramp, my heart pounding. Though I had just witnessed Bear flying down it, what Marco was asking seemed *impossible*. Troy whimpered, utterly terrified. We couldn't go back—the ground was too far below us. Going forward seemed just as perilous.

"Troy! Zeus!"

Trembling, I put one foot, then the other, on the slippery slide.

ART #1 TK

Two

As soon as my front paws touched the smooth ramp, everything went *wrong*! My feet slid forward and I collapsed, spinning. Frantically, I splayed out my claws, but they didn't slow me down one bit. Stinging water splashed into my eyes and I couldn't see and I fell faster and faster and—*sploosh!*—hit the pool. I struggled, sinking, water gushing up my nose.

I felt Marco's strong hands reaching for me. "Oh, Zeus," he crooned, "that was amazing."

Marco called and called for Troy, who bowed and wagged and turned in circles high up on the platform. Finally, Marco went up and carried my brother back down the steps. Why hadn't I thought of that?

Marco and I took several more trips down the slide. I didn't like it—I *hated* it—but I went because it made Marco so happy. Troy waited for us at the bottom and jumped on me as soon as Marco lifted me out of the pool.

"Let's get the chlorine out of your fur," Marco finally suggested. We all followed him gleefully, but we lost our enthusiasm when he turned a hose on us, dousing us with clear water.

Why? Weren't we already wet enough?

We were still soggy when Marco put us back in the crate. Even with the outdoor smells and Bear next to us, my brother and I dropped into an exhausted sleep the moment we started moving.

When we jerked to a halt, Marco pulled us out and set us on the ground. We were back in our yard, and I saw immediately that the family we'd met before had gathered right there on the grass, sitting cross-legged as if waiting for us to arrive.

Troy and I ran to them joyfully. I had already started to love Marco, and he knew of the most amazing places to take a dog. But he was just one person. This was several boys and several girls and a man and a woman. They were a *family*. I wanted to be with *them*.

Plus, I could feel that they already loved me completely. Marco liked me, and he liked that I'd gone down the slide with him. But as Bear came out of his crate and sat loyally by Marco's side, I realized that Marco already had a dog, and that dog was not me, or Troy either.

"Aloha, Mr. 'Ōpūnui," Marco called out cheerfully.

Roger was there too, smiling. "Aloha, Marco. Got a couple of anxious people here."

The children were giving Troy and me so much love we were wriggling in absolute delight.

"Which one is ours?" the woman asked urgently. "Were you able to decide which one you want to keep?"

Marco nodded at the woman. "Well," he corrected her kindly, "not *keep*, exactly. I train them to be water rescue dogs and sell them to overseas buyers."

"Overseas?" the man repeated.

"We don't really use dogs for water rescue here in the USA," Marco explained. "Scarborough, in Maine, is the only place I know about. But it's a big thing in Europe." He glanced over to where Troy and I were being cuddled by the children. "These are both great dogs, two of the best pups I've seen at this age. But Zeus was absolutely fearless. I can see him diving out of a hovering helicopter someday, hitting the water in heavy surf, and pulling a swimmer to safety. So it'll be Zeus that I'm taking."

I heard my name and felt the approval from Marco. I figured he was telling the family that I was the best dog and the one that should go with them.

So I was startled when the woman turned and called, "It's Troy!" Everyone in the family immediately surrounded my brother, petting him, showering him with kisses while he licked their faces in response. The children were smiling and giggling and happy. "You're our dog. You're our dog," a boy kept saying.

The girl who was holding me got up from where we were sitting together in the grass. Gently, she put me at Marco's feet.

I licked Marco's toes so he wouldn't feel left out and turned around to hurry back to my new family. But he put a hand down to my collar and held me still.

I was dumbfounded when, a few moments later, a boy, staggering a little under my brother's weight, led his whole family out the gate. I stayed behind with Marco. I didn't have a choice.

When the gate closed behind the family, I realized that the last glance from my brother might be all that I would ever have of him. Just as my sisters and other brothers and my mother had been led out into the world by their people, Troy had been taken by his.

What about me? I gazed up at Marco. Though he was approving and smiling and friendly, I did not get the sense that he had fallen in love with me the way the children had fallen for Troy.

Did that mean I would never have a person of my own?

"Come on, Zeus," Marco announced, "let's go home."

I was back in the crate soon after. There was plenty of my brother's odor in the carpet under my feet, but he was gone.

From his own crate nearby, Bear glowered at me, apparently disappointed to see me. I slept but awoke instantly when the vibration shuddered to a stop. We were not home, we were not at the place with the pools and the river and the slide—we were someplace else. Strong, humid odors filled my nose—wet plants, mud, water. *Moving* water—I could hear it.

Marco's hands gathered me and tenderly set me in some grass. I squatted, and then Marco lifted me up and climbed the steps of a house. Bear trotted ahead of us through the front door.

"Look at this baby!" a woman's voice crooned. A very large woman with delicious-smelling hands reached for me. She was as tall as Marco but moved more massively through the world. Her white teeth gleamed against her dark skin as she beamed at me.

"Tutu, this is Zeus. He's going to live with us for a while."

The woman (Tutu?) laughed as I licked her face. "Zeus!"

"Did you hear from my son?" Marco asked the wonderful woman.

"Kimo landed. He's on the airport shuttle. He should be here in ten minutes or so," she replied, as she set me down.

Marco grinned. "Can't wait to show him his birthday present!"

I wanted to add to the joy, so I raced around the

house, my nose down, then turned on Bear, nipped at his ear, and dashed away. He didn't seem to realize how much fun we were having.

I was delighted when Marco fed Bear some delicious-smelling food in a bowl and gave me a more bland meal in a smaller bowl. We both choked down our food. Then I trotted over to Bear's bowl to see what he'd left for me and was disappointed to find nothing. Here I was, a new dog in the house, and I wasn't even being given a welcome gift.

To amuse myself, I found a shelf full of tasteless paper things and pulled one out and began shredding it. "*No,*" Marco shouted.

I was startled. I had never heard such a word, nor such a tone from a human. I looked at Bear for an explanation and he glared back as if I'd done something wrong. What was a No?

"Don't chew the books, Zeus," Marco scolded me. I lowered my head and let my ears sink down.

"Kimo's shuttle is right around the corner!" Tutu announced.

"I'm going to put the dogs behind the gate in the back room until the boy's settled," Marco told her. I jumped up when Marco called, "Bear!," and I followed the big dog down the hall into a room that was shut off with a gate.

Bear gave me a glum look. He seemed to think that whatever was happening was my fault.

Marco closed us in and left us alone. Bear sat expectantly at the gate, so I did too. We both sprang into alertness when we heard the sounds of excited voices. Another human male had arrived.

"Tutu Nani!" the new male called. His voice sounded younger than Marco's.

"Aloha, Kimo! It's so good to have you back."

Bear and I were pressed firmly against the gate. I noticed that the spaces between the slats were wide—puppy width, in fact. I pushed my little nose into the gap and then wriggled my body until I was out.

Bear glared in disapproval, but he was on the other side of the gate, and I knew he was just jealous that he couldn't do what I had done. I scampered down the hall toward those voices, gaining speed.

"How was your birthday?" Marco asked.

"Great!" came the reply. "Mom gave me a basketball."

"I've got something for you too," Marco advised with a smile.

I slid around the corner and saw a young male talking to Marco. The new boy caught the motion and turned, lighting up in a smile. "Oh wow," he blurted, "you got me a puppy!"

The boy fell to his knees and held out his hands and I jumped into them. It was as glorious as jumping from the banks of the river into the water next to Marco, a plunge that took me from the life I'd had to the life I was going to have. This was, I realized, why I was here. *This* was my boy!

"Oh," Marco murmured.

The boy was grinning and I was trying to lick his face. He was pulling his mouth out of the way. "What's his name?"

"Zeus."

"Oh, Zeus. Zeus," the boy gasped, still laughing.

Marco cleared his throat. "Actually, no, that's not your birthday present."

The boy struggled to his feet. I tried to go with him, tried to stay in his arms, but he let me slip gently down to the floor. I dove onto his feet, chewing at a leather strap I found across his ankle.

"No, this is your present." Marco dug behind the couch and pulled up a long, white board.

"Oh," the boy exclaimed, "you, uh, you got me a new surfboard! Amazing! Yeah, thanks, Dad!"

"Happy birthday, Kimo," Tutu called from her side of the room. "Thirteen—a big teenager now!"

Marco came over to us. I wagged but I was still gazing up at the boy.

Marco was not my person, but this boy was different. We looked into each other's eyes and I could *feel* it. Every dog has a person. This one was mine.

"Zeus isn't going to live with us permanently," Marco explained to him. "You know how this works, Kimo.

ART #2 TK

Every eighteen months or so I bring on a new pup, train it, then I sell it at auction to be a water rescue dog. It's part of what I do for a living."

The boy was still grinning at me, and when he put his hand down, the love flowed into me and I wagged as hard as I could.

"Kimo," Marco warned. The boy glanced up. Marco shook his head. "Don't get attached to this dog. We're not keeping Zeus. He has a bigger purpose. He's a working dog."

It was very strange to feel some sadness in this boy, my boy, even while I was licking his fingers and he was scratching behind my ears with just the right pressure. I knew I would have to love him as hard as I could to make that sadness go away.

A little later, I followed Bear to a table and mimicked him while he sat, an attentive expression on his face. The air was alive with food smells wafting from the table, and Marco, Tutu, and Kimo pulled up chairs. Bear seemed to believe that people eating meant dogs would soon be eating, too. I wasn't going to question his wisdom.

"Are you ready for school Monday?" Tutu asked Kimo. "I guess it's always so hard to go back after spring break. Maybe just realize everybody feels the same way. Probably even the teachers. Was it strange to go back home?"

Marco looked up from his plate. "*This* is Kimo's home," he observed quietly.

Tutu nodded patiently. "Yes, that's what I mean."

Kimo shrugged. "It's always fun to see my friends, and it's so different there. The rain's cold. We went to Eagle Creek reservoir but the water was *freezing*. Oh, and you know how here we call everyone Auntie and Uncle, even if we're not really related? They don't do that there unless somebody's an actual uncle. Or aunt."

Tutu sniffed. "Unfriendly and disrespectful."

Kimo grinned. "I missed you, Tutu Nani."

I started to think this nice woman was called Tutu Nani and not just Tutu. It seemed to fit—she was solid and needed a bigger name than most people.

Marco was gazing at Kimo with a warm smile. "It's so good to have you back, son. There's just so much more . . . I don't know . . . *life* when you're around."

"Thanks, Dad."

"I agree," Tutu Nani added.

"What did you do for Prince Jonah Kūhiō Kalanianaʻole Day?" Kimo asked her.

"Went kayaking up the coast, just like every year," she responded.

Marco frowned slightly. "Though I asked her not to. I worry about you, Tutu."

Tutu Nani waved her hand dismissively. "How's your

mother?" she asked Kimo. There was a little hesitation in her voice.

"I think Mom's happy," Kimo replied. "She seems happy."

Tutu Nani shook her head and scowled a little. "Indianapolis is no place for my daughter. She should come back home. She should live here, and be with *ohana*, with family."

"Sure, but the company she bought is in Indiana," Kimo pointed out.

"Then she should sell it back," Tutu Nani answered primly.

Kimo's hand stealthily lowered, tossing a few morsels down for the dogs. Bear's instincts were *perfect*! I leaped on one chunk of soft bread while the big dog lapped up another.

I heard an odd noise and Marco stood and pressed a rectangular object to his face—later, I would learn to think of it as a phone. He spoke, then looked at Bear, who went alert, sensing something. "You ready to work, Bear?"

"What's happening?" Kimo asked.

"A lost hiker," Marco explained, "Last seen up at the trailhead by the Waimea River. No sign of him."

"Can we come too, Dad?" Kimo asked. "Zeus and me?"

Marco hesitated. "I don't know."

"But Dad," Kimo argued, "there's no school. It's still

technically spring break. I can stay out as late as we need."

I wagged, because Marco turned his gaze down on me. "All right," he decided finally. "Let's show Zeus what we're all about."

Three

A short time later, I charged out the front door with Bear to the thing everyone called the Jeep. I could see it a little better now, and I noticed that it had no ceiling and no side windows and, of course, the two crates in the back. I watched jealously as Bear leaped up under his own power and slid into his crate while I waited impatiently for Kimo to pick me up and put me in mine.

I was so excited I was trembling. Bear watched me wearily as I panted and paced and yipped. I had no idea what we were doing, but since Marco and Kimo were with us, I knew it was going to be so much *fun*!

We drove quite a distance and many odors came to me along the way. A salty, thick smell flowed from one direction, while the fragrance of dirt and flowers came from the other. Soon, the Jeep stopped in a flat area with several parked cars, and Kimo took me out. I ran around, wagging and sniffing, and scarfed up a stale piece of bread I found under a bush. This was an amazing place, wherever it was.

Bear seemed unimpressed. His eyes were focused on Marco. I thought Bear could probably use a good session with a squeaky toy. He should learn to relax a little.

We followed Marco down a narrow dirt path to where a group of people stood by loud, rushing waters. The people all turned at our approach and a woman broke from the crowd and ran to us, wiping tears from her face. "Oh thank God, thank God," she sobbed as she reached us. "Can your dog find my brother, Brent?"

"We're going to try, ma'am," Marco replied gravely.

"I don't know how I would live without Brent. He's the only family I have left!"

The rest of the people, all men, joined us. They were, of course, happy to see me. I did my best to entertain them, flopping on my back for a tummy rub, licking their hands, and racing around their feet.

"That pup's got a lot of energy," one man observed dryly.

I ran to Kimo, inviting him to play, but he wanted to stand around and do nothing.

"How old's your brother?" Marco asked the sad woman.

"He's sixty-eight," the woman answered frantically. "And he's not in good shape. He has a heart condition.

Something awful must have happened! He's been missing for *hours*."

Marco turned to the rest of the people. "Where's the PLS, does anybody know?"

"PLS?" a man asked.

"Place last seen," Marco explained.

"Oh, yes. Well, there's his car." The man waved a hand. "We thought maybe he crossed the stream here. He could have misjudged how deep the water is, after all the rain in the mountains."

Marco looked up at the sky. "Getting dark." He glanced at the sad woman, who was biting her lip. "You brought the clothes?" The woman nodded and Marco accepted the bundle of clothing she thrust forward.

"Bear," Marco called sharply. "Scent."

Bear came running over as if Marco had just opened a can of dog food, shoving his snout into the clothing. I took a shot at it too, sticking my nose up there. I couldn't see the value in any of it.

"All right," Marco commanded. "Bear. Search."

"Oh God, *please* find him!" the woman added urgently.

Bear immediately took off running. A running dog is very hard to resist, so I made to follow, but Kimo snagged my collar, and moments later he snapped a leash onto it. I pulled and twisted and whined, drawing a frown from Marco. "Stay, Zeus," Kimo commanded.

I didn't know what a Stay was and I wanted to dash around, like Bear!

Bear trotted along, sometimes sticking his nose up in the air, sometimes putting it down to the ground. I watched in complete befuddlement as he plunged into the fast-moving waters. Hadn't we already done enough of that kind of thing today?

Immediately, despite his strong shoulders, Bear began to drift downstream. But he kept swimming steadily, focused on reaching the opposite shore.

The man standing next to Marco shook his head. "We already searched over there and didn't find any trace."

Marco put his fingers to his lips and let loose a high, piercing whistle. "Bear!" he called.

I watched Bear. He was not responding to Marco. By now he'd clambered out of the river on the far side, and he continued to course back and forth, his nose high and then low. Obviously, he was looking for something. Had they hidden some treats over there?

Marco lifted his fingers and made the same ear-shattering noise. When he yelled, "Bear!," Kimo's voice joined his. Marco put his hands on his hips and shook his head. "He's never done that before. It's like he can't hear me. Let's all try it."

I was startled and amazed when every human put hands to their mouth and yelled, *"Bear!"*

Bear jerked his head around. Marco lifted his arm straight up, then waved it back, and Bear returned across that swift stream. As Bear climbed out and then shook his dripping coat, Marco gestured with the same hand, pointing down the bank. Bear responded by wheeling and heading in that direction.

We waited expectantly, though for what, I had no idea. Marco pulled out his phone and stared at it. The sky was starting to darken overhead, and Marco's face glowed in the light from the screen.

"What's that?" the sad woman asked.

"It's an app connected to the camera on Bear's vest. It's a pretty jerky image, but we can see what's going on. When he finds your brother, he'll stop and we'll get a good look and see if there's anything wrong. And the way Bear's moving, he's got the scent."

"He can smell somebody in the water?" the sad woman asked.

Marco grinned. "He's a trained water rescue dog. That's what they do."

More time passed. I kept yanking and straining at the leash, wanting to follow Bear and see if I was right about those hidden treats. Then Kimo picked me up, and I squirmed and licked his face.

"Zeus needs to calm down," Marco commented. He glanced down. "Bear's close. He's moving in a straight line now. Any second."

Everyone tensed. I yawned. Then Marco brightened. "There he is! Got him!" He held his phone out to the sad woman, who gasped. "He's wet," Marco pointed out, "but he's up on shore, lying down. In a minute, Bear will come running back to give us the good news."

The woman began weeping in great, shuddering gusts. I smelled the salt on her face. Marco put a hand on her shoulder. "I know that was tough to look at, especially with the camera bleaching out all the color, but your brother's alive. I can see that his leg's broken, but he's definitely breathing, and he's not even shivering." He turned to the other men. "I'm going to need my inflatable splints, a C collar, and a stretcher. We'll carry him back to this parking lot for helicopter evacuation."

I looked up, because I smelled Bear coming, and sure enough, within moments he came crashing out of the bushes and ran straight to Marco.

I expected Marco to smile at Bear, pet him, maybe even wrestle a little with him on the ground, but they both were all business. "Bear, Reveal!" Marco commanded. Bear immediately turned to trot away again, moving slowly, and now we all followed. Kimo put me down so I could walk next to him, which was something Bear didn't seem to understand—that a dog should stay next to his person. Why would Bear walk off like that, abandoning Marco? I thought this was a dog who did not deserve any treats at all.

Bear kept glancing back to check if we were still there. "Reveal," Marco would say each time, and Bear would resume his slow trot. There were a lot of bushes that the people had to push through, but they did so rapidly, tracking Bear.

Our path led us along the river. It was moving very fast, and in the failing light it looked dark and rather frightening. "All right," Marco announced. "We're close."

He picked up his pace, and the rest of us did the same. Soon, I could smell someone, a wet someone, up ahead. Bear had stopped moving. I could smell that, too.

I stayed on his scent, though, pulling Kimo toward where the big dog was waiting. I was pretty sure that we were trying to locate him. This was probably something Bear did a lot. He would run off, get lost, and then it would be up to dogs like me to find him.

Finally, we stumbled on both Bear and the man I had been smelling. He sat up as the sad woman ran to him. "Easy, Monica," the man murmured. She threw her arms around him and I could feel so many emotions pouring off her that it was hard to sort them out. This man, I realized, was very important to this woman.

Marco knelt by the man, touching him gently. The man winced. "Your leg's broken, I'm afraid," Marco told him. "And you're bleeding from the scalp."

The man nodded. "I tripped over a root, if you can believe it. I knew I was in trouble when I hit the water. All I could do was keep my head up. Man, that current moves faster than you'd believe. I grabbed at some low-hanging branches and pulled myself here. I was trying to make it to a road, but this was as far as I could get."

"You did great," Marco assured him.

After that, a lot of things happened that I found completely bewildering. Marco wrapped the man's leg so that it was held out straight. Then they put him on a kind of thin, flat bed. Marco and the other men each picked up a corner of it. With Bear up front and Kimo, the sad lady, and me all following, we slowly made our way back through the brush.

Occasionally, the man would wince, and once he let out a small cry, and I could feel pain breaking inside him when he did so. Finally, we hit a wide path, and then we were back with the cars. One of the men took a large toy off his belt and murmured into it. Then he turned to Marco. "Chopper'll be here any minute."

Bear and I raised our heads as a heavy, pulsing sound came to us. The people weren't reacting, so perhaps they couldn't hear it, but I could tell something very loud was headed our way. Bear's ears dropped—he didn't like the noise.

I was mystified when I saw a big machine rushing toward us *in the air*. It centered itself over the wide parking lot, making a pounding, thundering noise, beams of light flashing down to the ground. Gradually, it settled down in the gravel. I blinked and huddled close to Kimo's feet as a wind blew sand in my face.

Marco and his friends lifted the wet man and carried him to this strange, loud machine. They stuffed him in like Kimo shoving me in the dog crate, stood back, and waved as the machine, making a huge racket, lifted ponderously into the air and flew off.

Bear watched all this from behind the Jeep, his ears down. I trotted over to him to seek an explanation, sensing that he was upset. He perked up, though, when we were given treats. Mine was turkey! Kimo fed me into my crate and Bear jumped into his.

Marco buckled in but the Jeep didn't move. "I brought you along to see Bear in action so you'd understand the point I've been making, Kimo," I heard him say.

"The point?"

Marco nodded gravely. "Bear's trained in water rescue, but dogs don't do that in Hawaii, so I made him a search and rescue dog. A *working* search and rescue dog. He earns his keep." Marco glanced back at me and I wagged, though I was watching Kimo. "Zeus is going to be water rescue."

"You trained Bear, but you didn't sell him."

"Right," Marco agreed. "I couldn't sell Bear at the end of the program because he failed the helicopter test." He sighed. "It's so difficult. You can train a dog to jump off the platform. You can train the dog to rescue people from the water. But a key element is to leap out of a hovering helicopter into the ocean to save drowning people." Marco twisted in his seat to gaze at Bear, who thumped his tail. "Bear was so intimidated by the noise, he became confused. He did jump, but he couldn't find the person who was pretending to drown. He swam in circles. He just couldn't get past it. We tried and tried, but eventually I had to fail him. Otherwise," Marco went on, "I would have sold him, Kimo. I promise. That was the plan."

"And you always stick to the plan," Kimo noted, a little sourly.

Marco grinned sheepishly. "People have said that about me, I will admit."

Kimo was unhappy. I sensed it and whimpered a little, wanting him to know I was right there. When his gaze found mine, I wagged.

I knew that *he* knew that he was my person, and that I was his dog. That was enough to make me very happy. It should have done the same for him.

Four

My life made perfect sense. I was meant to be with Kimo and he was meant to be with me. That night I slept on his bed with my head on his chest as if he were my brother Troy, but I kept waking up, so overcome with affection I couldn't help but gnaw on Kimo's ear. He pushed me away each time, but there was love even in that action.

The next day we played in the grass. Bear was there, watching this whole thing with his usual dour expression. How he could resist when Kimo tossed a bouncing ball in his direction, I had no idea, but I was so focused on getting to the toy that I didn't have time to waste pondering Bear's problems. He was just a dog who didn't understand how to have fun.

Sometimes, when was standing so still, I couldn't help but run over and jump at his face. But he usually just held his head up out of my reach and waited for me to hurry back to Kimo.

I expected every day to be the same, but the next morning Marco appeared in the doorway and said, "Kimo," and my boy groaned and sat up. "It's 6:52."

"6:52," Kimo mumbled. "Not 6:45. Not even 6:50. That's my dad."

I loved hearing his voice.

It was very early. Tutu Nani stood in the wonderful room called Kitchen, making both noises and delicious odors. It was in the kitchen that morning that I learned the words *breakfast* and *bacon*, giving me even more reasons to love Kimo.

Marco and Bear left in the Jeep, meaning I had the kitchen and its wonderful smells all to myself!

Tutu Nani looked up when a car horn sounded from the direction of the driveway. "Well, you better get going," she told Kimo kindly.

Kimo dropped to his knees and took a breath. "Okay. I'm going to go to school now, Zeus."

Whatever that was, I was ready! After he'd rubbed my ears, he got back up, and I confidently padded behind his heels until, so suddenly I didn't know how to react, he slipped out the front door and shut it firmly behind him.

"He's just gone to school. He'll be home soon, I promise," Tutu Nani sang to me.

I had no idea what she was saying and I wasn't fooled by the happy tone of her voice. My boy had vanished. Kimo was gone. *Forever.* This was the worst thing that could happen to a dog. I cried, letting my fear and pain pour out through my voice.

Tutu Nani came to me and, grunting, lowered herself onto the floor. She reached for me, gathering me into a secure, warm hug. She was so much bigger than Kimo! I stopped whimpering, comforted by her embrace. "It's all going to be okay, little one," she murmured. The love flowed through her strong arms, lulling me into a deep sleep.

Eventually, she slid me out of her lap and I awoke. Kimo was still not there. "I have to make my leis," Tutu Nani informed me. "Would you like to sit with me?"

I heard the question, and when she sat at a table, I decided to flop onto her feet. A powerful smell of flowers filled my nose.

"I make them for the hotel. They hand them out to guests. My Tutu taught me, but I make my own designs. See? They're very popular."

I glanced up drowsily. She was holding down a rope of flowers. I resolved to chew it later—I was too tired to bother right now, and still sad because Kimo wasn't there.

I roused myself from a lazy nap when my ears picked up the rumble of the Jeep. I heard heavy thuds, smelled Bear, then Marco, then an unknown person . . . then Kimo! I raced to the door and tackled him the moment he stepped inside, sobbing, kissing him. Then, full of joy, I raced around the room, jumping on chairs, skidding on rugs, banging my face into a corner of the couch, but not letting that slow me down for a moment.

"Wow, that's . . . there's a lot of spirit in that dog," Marco commented, sounding a little concerned.

There was a third person, a female child Kimo's age, who clapped her hands. "Puppy!"

I ran to her. "This is Cousin Giana, Zeus," Kimo advised me.

"Hi, Zeus! I'm the smart one in the family," the girl greeted me, grinning with delight.

"Giana's the only person in history to be kicked off the debate team for arguing," Kimo informed me.

"That's not even close to what happened," the girl countered.

Eventually, with everyone calling the girl Giana, I figured this was her name. She smelled wonderfully of flowers, and though her skin, hair, and eyes were all as light as Marco's, her smile matched Kimo's almost exactly. I could sense that Kimo and Tutu and Marco loved Giana, so I loved her too. It seemed to me she could be a good friend to a dog.

Giana joined the rest of the family for dinner, and my hunch proved correct: she was very good at handing down secret treats to the deserving dogs under the table. "When do you start training Zeus?" she asked Marco. "And could you train Kimo at the same time?"

I snapped my attention to Giana at the sound of my name.

"Training this little one is going to be a challenge," Marco replied bleakly. "I like a high-energy dog, but this one might be a tad too rambunctious. He might fail."

There was a long silence. "Well," Kimo countered cautiously, "would that be so bad? If he failed training, he'd still be a wonderful dog."

Marco firmly shook his head. "That's not an option. We don't have the money for dog food, and especially vet bills. Bear's keep is paid for with donations, usually from the families of people he's rescued. We just don't have room in our budget for a pet, Kimo."

I sensed that Kimo was unhappy. I went to lick his feet.

"I don't make much as a paramedic," Marco continued. "Training water rescue dogs gives me the income that allows us to live here."

Tutu Nani snorted. "You know you don't have to pay me rent."

"Yes, I do, Tutu," Marco replied evenly.

Tutu Nani turned to Giana. "Your uncle Marco is an honorable man, but I tell him, when I sold the land and kept this house, I wound up with the best place in Hawaii—right off the river, here in the mountains!—and no mortgage."

"Being an adult means paying your own way," Marco insisted.

"Plus," Giana said into the awkward silence, "Uncle Marco's got the most organized flower garden in Hawaii. It's like the plants are in the *army*."

The people relaxed. "I do like things to be organized," Marco acknowledged. He focused on Kimo. "Tell you what. It's almost April, and in the summer we always wind up working a lot of overtime in Search and Rescue. How about I put you in charge of Zeus's basic training? Sit, Heel, Drop, Stay. *Especially* Stay. Stay teaches focus and temperament. It's going to be hard for such a spirited dog to learn, but you can do it. Start with Sit."

Kimo grinned. "I would love that, Dad!"

"And, when you work with a dog, your relationship changes," Marco added. "Zeus will go from being a pet to being a project. This'll make it easier for you to accept when we send Zeus to auction."

Kimo's smile faded.

"When's that? The auction?" Giana inquired.

"It's always in August, so a little less than fifteen months."

"I'll help train," Giana volunteered.

Marco smiled. "Sounds like a plan."

Soon after that, a car pulled up in the driveway and Giana raced out the door. Everyone went to bed, except Marco, who sat in a chair and rustled papers. They didn't seem as though they'd be any good to chew on, so I elected to gnaw on Bear's ears, which he didn't appreciate. He even *growled*, which was, I felt, a bit of an overreaction. I was a puppy, after all. My mouth was on fire. I needed to chew on something, and his body parts were the only things available that didn't earn me the word *No*.

Then I remembered that Kimo had shown me a squeaky toy earlier. I attacked it, creating glorious noises.

Marco sighed. "Really, Zeus?"

When Bear fell asleep, I left the toy and snoozed against him, comfortable. In that moment I realized something. I didn't just love Kimo. I also loved Bear.

What I didn't love was the word *school*, which meant that Kimo left me. It was even worse because Bear and Marco usually went out of the door at around the same time. But Tutu Nani was kind and cuddled me and gave me treats to help me get through it, and after several days I figured out something wonderful: *Kimo always came back!*

"We'll start working on training soon, Zeus. Next month," Kimo promised me. "When you're maybe a little more calm."

I discovered a river in our backyard, beyond the fence, a shallow stream full of rocks and wonderful scents. When Kimo came home from school we always ran to the fence to smell it. We were standing there together when I heard Tutu Nani approach.

"What's wrong, honey?" Tutu Nani asked softly. "I can tell something's bothering you."

Kimo gave her a bleak look. "You heard Dad. We're selling Zeus a year from August. No matter what. It's the *plan.*"

"Well," Tutu Nani replied after reflecting for a moment, "your father gets upwards of twelve thousand dollars for each dog. That's a lot of money to a family like ours. It keeps us in groceries. You'll understand when you get older, but sometimes you have to do whatever it takes to feed your family."

"I don't care," Kimo snapped.

Tutu Nani folded her arms. "I understand that you're upset, but that doesn't give you the right to speak to me in those tones."

Kimo lowered his eyes. "Sorry, Tutu," he muttered. The disturbed emotions pouring off him were so strong I licked his bare leg and thought about whining a little, to share in the way he was feeling. "But Dad says that by training him I'll be okay with giving up my dog. That it'll be *fun.*" His lips twisted bitterly. "But I just want Zeus to stay with me."

"I understand," Tutu Nani murmured. "Would it . . . would it maybe be a good idea if you did what your father suggested, and see Zeus as a project instead of a pet? Stop letting him sleep on your bed, before it's too late?"

Kimo sighed. "It's already too late, Tutu Nani. I love Zeus, and he loves me. I can't let Dad sell him. I just can't."

Some mornings no one said "school" and everyone remained in bed even after the frogs sang, which is when Marco's feet would usually thud around the house. I was always so overjoyed I jumped on Kimo's head. "Get off, you crazy dog! There's no school! You do this every weekend!" he'd groan. I didn't know what he was saying, but I hoped it had something to do with bacon.

After breakfast, Bear and I would follow Kimo into the yard. The stream gurgled, birds sang, and the sun poured down, warming the flowers and convincing them to fill the air with their fragrances. I was with my boy and happy.

"Okay," he declared. "It's May. I've put this off long enough. Time to get to it."

After that, Kimo started saying "Sit" to me. I did not know what a Sit was and preferred to chew on sticks.

Kimo kept saying it, though, and the tantalizing smell of a treat wafted from his closed fist. "Sit," he told me. He gave my butt a gentle push, so I resisted, thinking he was telling me that I was letting my tail drag on the ground. It wasn't fair for him to withhold that treat until I lifted my tail, but humans don't have tails and might not understand how it works.

ART #3 TK

"Sit," he instructed again.

I looked over at Bear, who, upon hearing this command, had planted his rear end firmly on the floor and was now staring expectedly at Kimo. "Good dog. Okay, Release," Kimo told him. Bear jumped up wagging, and accepted a bacon treat from Kimo.

We played this game over and over and over. It was no fun at all, and I was frustrated. Bear was being handed fistfuls of bacon treats and I was getting *nothing*.

After a little while, a memory came to me. At that place with the strange-smelling water and the slide, I'd followed Bear and done what he did. That had seemed to make Marco happy. Maybe it would be a good idea now?

I set my butt on the ground.

"Yes! Good dog," Kimo sang happily, *finally* giving me a treat.

I learned that the process of Kimo teaching me to obey his words was called Work. We did Sit Work a lot, and Drop Work, and Retrieve Work. (That was my favorite! He'd throw a ball and I'd bring it back.) For other fun Work, there was also Come and Shake (I held up my paw and Kimo yanked at it and then gave me chicken). Day after glorious day passed, most of them with School, all of them with Work.

Then one day he announced, "Okay, Dad says this is the most important one. Zeus. . . . Stay!"

And with that Kimo ran around and around in the

yard, waving his arms and calling, "Stay! Stay!" I followed, joyously leaping up on him as we dashed in circles.
"Good dog!"

Stay was the best Work of all!

I smelled Giana after a while and saw her step outside
into the backyard with us. "Stay. Stay," Kimo kept yelling, racing around, flapping his arms and tossing toys.
I heard Giana laughing, and so did Kimo. He stopped
instantly, whirling, and then his shoulders dropped.
"Oops," he murmured softly.

"What're you doing?" Giana asked curiously.

Five

I bounded over to greet Giana, and Kimo followed more slowly. Her eyebrows were raised. "Well?"

"So . . . I'm sort of training Zeus to screw up," Kimo explained sheepishly. "Bear lives with us because he failed the helicopter test. I figure if I can get Zeus to fail the command Stay, then Dad won't be able to sell him."

Giana laughed. "Well, it's a plan. A really dumb plan, but a plan."

"My dad says that Stay is the foundation for all the commands to dogs. It means the dog has surrendered its will to me. That's how he said it."

"It looks to me like Zeus has surrendered his will to chewing on a stick."

"Very funny. I'm just saying that when my dad sees what Zeus does when he's told to stay, he'll give up on the idea of Zeus becoming a water rescue dog."

"If you say so." Giana shrugged. "So school's out and day camp doesn't start until after July fourth. Why don't we show Zeus the beach?"

Well, the next thing that happened was more wonderful than anything in my life up to that point (except, of course, coming to live with my boy). Kimo slid me into a new vest and I followed him and Giana down the street, feeling the rough sidewalk under my pads and sniffing all the black rock walls in people's yards, artfully lifting my leg on some of them.

Then we sat on a bench. "Ready for a bus ride?" Giana asked me, and I wagged.

One of Kimo's friends pulled up in a huge, noisy car! Doors flapped open and we leaped aboard.

"Aloha," greeted the woman driving. "New service puppy, Kimo?"

"Aloha, Eleu! Yep. This is Zeus!"

"Aloha, Zeus! My name is Eleu." She held out her hand. It tasted like fish. I decided I loved her.

We sat among a lot of people who were excited to greet me. "Can I pet your dog?" a woman asked. "I see he's working. I wouldn't want to interfere."

"It's fine," Kimo assured her. "He's not doing actual work yet."

"Kimo doesn't do actual work either," Giana told the lady with a grin.

As we moved, a steadily growing scent came to my nose—a salty, earthy, wet, *huge* odor.

We jumped down out of that big car and took a long walk on warm pavement, each step taking us closer to what turned out to be our destination—the most astounding pool imaginable. It was enormous and gave up the smell of fish and salt and birds and many, many other unknown odors, and it was loud, with moving water in huge, crashing waves.

"It's the ocean, Zeus!" Kimo told me.

My boy was happy, so I was happy. I ran straight for the big pool, delighting in the spray as I hit it. I started swimming, feeling the glorious waves lift me up and drop me down. I wasn't scared of moving water this time—I remembered how I'd swum with Marco and Bear when I was younger, and how the moving water might dunk me but couldn't sink me.

"Zeus, you crazy dog," Kimo called with a laugh. "Come back."

I loved hearing my name, so I turned around. On the way back in, a wave gathered behind me and thrust me forward very rapidly, spraying salty water up my nose. I staggered out onto the sand, sneezing and shaking my head.

We played Stay all day in that water, racing around, leaping, swimming, splashing. Several people came up to greet me.

"How old's your puppy?" one of them asked.

"Kimo's thirteen but he's very immature," Giana answered.

Kimo rolled his eyes. "Around six months now," he said.

All the people I met gave me love, and though they weren't my boy and obviously didn't know my name, I loved them back. "Mahalo," the people often told Kimo.

That wasn't my name either.

We eventually left the sand and found our way to a place where freshwater poured from a high faucet. I took a long drink. When Kimo picked me up, I assumed it was for cuddles, but instead he thrust me under the nozzle.

The water poured down on me and I gave my boy a miserable look. I had spent the day loyally doing whatever he wanted, and this was my reward?

"He looks like you are *torturing* him," Giana said with a laugh. "He's spent the whole *day* in the water. What's the difference?"

"It's just a bath, you silly dog!" Kimo hooted at me. I did not feel the word *bath* was worth learning, if it had anything to do with this despicable soaking.

When we were done I smelled so dull and boring that I yearned to go splashing into the ocean again and get some rich odors back on my fur, but Kimo led me into the parking lot. A woman waited with a vehicle I had learned was called Truck. She knelt to greet me. Of course I ran to her. This was a place where everyone knew how to give love to a dog.

Kimo called the woman Auntie Adriana, while Giana called her Mom. People often seemed to get names wrong like this, just the way Marco was Marco to everyone except Kimo, who usually said "Dad." But I didn't mind, because Auntie Adriana Mom Whoever had a treat in her pocket. She brushed her light hair (same color as Giana's) from her face and handed it to me. It was cheese flavored and absolutely wonderful.

Kimo put me in a crate on the backseat and sat next to me. The truck started moving. "Did you remember sunblock?" Auntie Adriana Mom asked Giana.

Giana sighed in reply. "Yes, but only once. We were having so much fun, I forgot." She looked back over her seat at us. "I'm so jealous of you, Kimo. You get so tan, but I just burn. It's my Italian heritage."

Kimo shrugged. "I'm part Italian, too, you know. Kimo *Ricci*."

"I'm so proud that you and Giana'll be counselors at day camp," Auntie Adriana Mom remarked. "Most kids spend summer vacation just playing."

"Not counselors," Kimo corrected. "Interns. Helpers. *Unpaid* helpers. But if they like us, we'll be hired next year, I hope."

"How could they not like you?"

At our driveway, Kimo and I jumped out. I squatted and then raced around, smelling to see if anything had changed. It wasn't any different than it had been before, and that was wonderful.

Inside the house, Tutu Nani's hands smelled as delicious as always. I licked her calves and she smiled down at me. Then she gave Kimo a long, long look. "Kimo, I was here when Giana came over. I was unpacking groceries."

"Okay," Kimo replied innocently. "Did you need help? Should I have come in?"

Tutu Nani shook her head. "No, but I overheard what you were saying. How you're training Zeus to fail at Stay."

Kimo went very still. Tutu Nani leaned forward, gazing deeply into his eyes. "You cannot win something good through dishonesty. Not even for love, Kimo. Understand me? You must always be truthful." She sighed. "In Hawaiian, we have a word—you've heard it. *Pono*."

Kimo looked away.

Tutu Nani put a hand on his shoulder. "No, please listen, I'm telling you something very important, because I love you, Kimo. Pono doesn't just mean honesty, or righteousness, or fairness. It's a way of life, of living with balance and integrity. And most of all it means hope, because while we all try to be honest all the time, it isn't easy. We hope, for our own sake, that we can move truthfully through the world. But this is different. This is a deliberate falsehood, isn't it? And those, Kimo, those will always, always wind up causing you more problems than they're worth."

"I'm sorry, Tutu. I'm just feeling . . . desperate. I

don't want to lose Zeus. I *can't.*" His voice was getting shaky, and I was worried about my boy. We'd had such a happy day. Why had his mood changed so suddenly?

"Ever since Mom moved away, I've been so . . ." Kimo stopped talking.

Tutu Nani sighed and reached out to envelop Kimo in a huge hug, and I did my best to help by wiggling between them and panting up at my boy. Slowly he became less sad. But he wasn't as happy as he'd been by the big salty pool, and so neither was I.

At dinner that night, Bear and I did Sit, being good dogs, deserving lasagna.

"How's training going?" Marco asked. "Has Zeus learned Stay yet?"

"We've been . . . working on that," Kimo answered carefully.

Marco grunted. "I'll take him out in a day or two, see how he's doing."

"Oh . . . kay," Kimo responded.

A lasagna treat came down. Sit was the most wonderful thing I had done in my life—not as active as the wildly fun Stay, but with far more treats.

"I'll bring home a coconut tomorrow," Tutu Nani decided. "Coconut flesh is very good for a dog."

Kimo was fast asleep, my head rising and falling on his chest, when I heard a low murmur coming from the living room. I jumped off the bed and padded out to see what was going on. I saw Bear lying on his side, his legs splayed, his tail twitching as Marco knelt over him.

"You are such a good dog, Bear," Marco was crooning in a whisper, "such a good, good dog. Please be okay. Please don't be going deaf."

I could feel the love pouring out of Marco and into Bear, and I could feel Bear's response, a good dog loving a person. I realized, in that moment, something I should have known all along: Marco was Bear's person. His *only* person. They loved each other and would always be together, just as I would always be together with Kimo

I turned, suddenly needing to be with my boy. I scampered down the hall, darted through his doorway, and leaped up onto bed. Kimo stirred and then came wide awake. When my tongue found his mouth, he sputtered, shaking his head, laughing. "What are you doing, you crazy dog?"

The next night after a dinner called Hamburgers (wonderful!), Marco and Kimo had a conversation in the kitchen, and then Kimo put both Bear and me on leashes. Bear's leash was long and mine was pretty short, which was the opposite of how it should be. I needed room to scamper and jump, especially if someone were to say "Stay." Bear just mostly stuck close to Marco's side.

Back in the living room, Kimo told us, "Sit," snapping his fingers. "Face me, Bear. Face me."

We didn't understand what he was saying, but we did understand that Kimo was waving a fist around that was giving off the unmistakable odor of those bacon treats, so of course we both paid attention.

"All right," I heard Marco murmur. I didn't turn. "Bear, Come." He was speaking softly. I heard the word *Come* and knew that one, but I was on leash, and anyway, Kimo had the bacon. "Bear," Marco repeated more loudly. "Bear."

Bear continued to stare at Kimo. "Come," Marco commanded, even more loudly. He clapped his hands quietly, and I turned my head toward him, wondering what he was up to. Bear glanced at me and realized something had caught my attention.

He twisted and saw Marco and immediately eased over to his person, wagging. That's how much Bear loved Marco—the dog was even willing to forgo *bacon*.

Marco gave Bear a kiss on the top of his head. "Oh, Bear," he murmured sadly. He glanced up at Kimo. "This is not good."

The next morning, Bear anxiously tracked Marco, sensing that something was worrying his person. I realized that the two of them were so in tune with each other that Bear could instantly tell when his person was about to alter his pattern. I didn't yet have this skill—to me, Kimo kept changing things at random, doing school, doing no school, doing Work. I hoped I would eventually figure it all out.

Several times I approached Bear and touched my nose to his to let him know that I understood he was upset and that I was willing to chew on a ball, or wrestle with him, or bite him in the face, if that would help.

"Are you going to take Bear to the vet for his hearing?" Kimo asked, as he and Marco ate cold milk splashed on something that smelled tasteless and sounded crunchy. I did Sit, figuring I might as well eat whatever it was if it was offered.

"Probably not," Marco replied. "I'll look into it, but I don't think there's much that can be done. The real question is whether he can still do S&R work. We'll see. Meanwhile, I'm taking Zeus today—giving Bear the day off." Marco smiled down at me.

When Marco put me on the leash and led me out the door, I figured I knew what had been bothering Bear, who watched forlornly through the screen door as his person lifted me into the crate. Somehow, Bear had sensed that I was going with Marco and he wasn't.

"All right, Zeus," Marco said as he closed the gate door on the crate. "Let's see how well you've mastered Stay."

Six

Later that day, after Marco and I had finished playing, I was in the backyard when Kimo slid the door open and he and Giana came out to see me. I ran to him so joyously I nearly knocked him over. "Whoa! Big dog!" he exclaimed. Marco came out to join us. Bear went to his person and Marco bent down and rubbed Bear's chest. "Hey, Dad," Kimo said.

"Aloha. Have you two started interning at day camp yet?"

Kimo shook his head. "I guess this year it's not until after Independence Day. Giana and I went snorkeling at Ka'ena Point. How was your day?"

In that moment, Marco seemed a little bit like Bear: dour and glum. He shook his head. "Zeus doesn't know Stay."

"Oh?" Kimo replied warily.

"Huh, that's odd," Giana added.

Marco gave them a wry grin. "It's the craziest thing. I've never seen anything like it. It's like a starting pistol going off. He went kind of berserk on me. Ran around barking and jumping on sticks."

"Well," Kimo observed cautiously, "we've been working on that, but he seems to have trouble understanding."

"Working *hard*," Giana interjected.

Marco nodded. "He's the most high-strung dog I've ever met. That's why I've always stuck with Newfoundlands, or in the case of Bear, setter/Newfoundland mix. Labradors can be like this, sometimes. They're great water dogs and they don't mind cold temperatures, but sometimes they're just too wild."

"Maybe," Kimo suggested, "that just means that Zeus will need a lot more training than we first thought. Maybe a year from August is too soon to think about selling him."

Marco gave Kimo a long searching look. "Actually, at this point, I'm afraid what we have here is a failed dog."

"Oh," Kimo replied carefully, glancing at Giana. "You mean like Bear?"

"No, not like Bear at all," Marco answered reprovingly. "Bear can do everything a water rescue and a search dog is expected to do, except for jumping from a helicopter. He's a real working dog."

"All right . . ." Kimo began, but his father held up a hand.

"I think this is beyond our ability to fix, especially when you start working at day camp, which means you won't have the time you'll need to discipline such a rambunctious dog. If I had a choice I'd start over with a different animal, but the shelter doesn't have any suitable puppies right now. So I've made a new plan. I know a woman in California who does the kind of intensive training Zeus needs. She's sent me a few of her dogs for search and rescue training in the past, so she owes me a few favors. We're going to send Zeus to her for a crash, six-month program on how to behave. She's really good. If anyone can calm down this animal, she can."

I glanced at Kimo, sensing a huge distress. "California? *Six months?*" He held out his hands, as if reaching for Marco. "That's forever."

Marco shook his head. "I don't think dogs track time the way we do, especially here or in California, where the seasons don't change much. A month goes by, two months—to a dog, it feels like a day, or an hour, or a year. They don't really care."

"Wait, no, forever for *me*. Please just give me more time, Dad. I know I'll be busy, but I'll work with Zeus every day."

I did not like hearing my name pronounced with such dismay, and I went to Kimo with my tail and ears down.

Marco pursed his lips. "You've *been* working with him. Zeus is bright but he's just too wild. All he wants to do is play."

"It's my fault. I've mostly been playing. Instead of training, I mean. But I'll get serious. I promise. Please?"

Marco sighed. "I called her. The dog trainer, I mean. Her name's Bonnie. She has an open slot October thirtieth, Kimo. This is the only way."

Kimo regarded Marco in alarm. "Could I *please* keep trying until October, though?" he pleaded.

"I feel like that's just going to make everything worse, son. I warned you about bonding with Zeus. It's not going to be any easier in October. That why I've decided we should find a foster family for him."

"But wait," Giana objected. "Finding a foster means some other dog won't have a place to live."

"Well . . ." Marco seemed to be thinking over what Giana had said.

"If your plan is for Zeus to be fostered, you should foster him *here*!" Giana went on forcefully.

"And meanwhile I'll keep working with him," Kimo insisted.

Marco grinned. "I should have known you'd be persuasive, Giana. You always are. All right, yes. Sure. Today's July first. That gives you four months to bring Zeus under control. But I have to caution you, Kimo, from what I've seen, it's beyond what we can do. People say some Labradors never calm down, and I think Zeus is one of those."

"Thank you, Dad." When Kimo turned and ran to the house, I followed, still feeling like I had somehow been bad. But I didn't know what I'd done, or how to make it better.

In his bedroom, Kimo put his face to my fur. "What did I do, Zeus?" he murmured into my ear. "Tutu was right. Being dishonest backfired on me. She's *always* right." He pulled away and stared into my face. "I don't want you to go to California for a half a year. When you came back, would you even remember me?"

Kimo was hurting. I licked him and pressed against him that night while he slept. I knew that whatever was wrong, I could fix it with a dog's love.

The next morning, Kimo took me into the backyard, his pocket bulging with treats. I was pleased that Bear had gone with Marco that morning—those treats would all be for me!

Kimo had me do Sit. I knew that one and got a treat. Then he backed away a few steps. "All right, we're going to change everything now," he warned me. He held up a hand, then dropped it, and, looking resigned said, "Zeus, *Stay.*"

Yes, the very word I wanted to hear! I burst from Sit position but was shocked, though not displeased, when Kimo lunged forward and seized me in a tight hug. I couldn't run, but this new variation on Stay gave me a lot of love from my boy." No, Zeus," he whispered. "No, you have to do it right, now."

I did not know why he seemed so sad.

What could I do? I decided that I would show the

same energy as I always had during Stay, no matter what the command.

When he told me, "Sit," I ran around barking. When he said, "Drop," I rolled on my back and then ran around barking. Running around and barking was a big part of Stay, and the thing that had always made my boy the happiest.

Except it didn't. Something bad had happened.

I brightened when Giana came out of the sliding door. I was hoping she could help cheer things up. She was carrying something dry and uninteresting that she handed to Kimo.

He looked at it blankly. "What is it?"

"It's a book."

"I know it's a book. But my birthday was a couple of months ago. You got me a card with a monkey on it saying 'I can tell what you'll look like when you turn thirty,' and you bought me flippers to replace the ones you stole."

"I didn't steal them. You said they were getting too small for you and gave them to me. For *my* birthday you got me gift certificates to a pizza place and went with me and ate most of the pizza."

"I was just making sure it was good enough for the birthday girl."

"Right." Giana nodded. "Well, it's not a gift. It's your dad's book. Want me to read the title to you, or can you manage?"

"*Training Your Labrador in Search and Rescue Techniques.*"

"Exactly. I looked online. S and R training is one of the best ways to help a dog focus and be calm. Get it?"

Kimo brightened. "I do get it! Great idea, Giana. Genius!"

"Thank you. I'm glad you finally get that I'm a genius."

"We should celebrate—do we have any pizza gift certificates left?"

"*We?* So it was a birthday gift to *us*?"

Kimo was grinning. "Okay, *you*. Do *you* have any pizza gift certificates?"

"Nope. *You* used them all up."

"I guess you'll just have to spend your allowance, then."

Kimo was happier—the dry thing from Giana had been just what was needed! If he threw it, I figured I would chase it like a ball.

He didn't throw it, but he sure treated it like a favorite toy, carrying it with him and looking at it often. He even took it when he and Giana walked with me up into the hills behind our home, eventually finding a moist, muddy path that led into widely spaced trees.

"Okay," Kimo announced, looking at the dry toy. "First step is to hold Zeus while I run ahead. Then you say, 'Zeus, Search,' and I'll call him."

Giana looked around. "Should I cover his eyes so he doesn't see where you go?"

Kimo shook his head. "No, at first we just want him to run straight for me."

Something was happening, and I was panting with excited anticipation. When Kimo trotted off I strained at the leash in Giana's hand, twisting and crying, and finally she figured out what to do. She clipped the leash off my harness and shouted, "Zeus, Search!"

At the same time, Kimo called my name, so I ran to him and then past him and then down into the stream and up on the muddy banks and through the trees and over rocks and back down to Kimo, who grabbed at me—a grabbing game! I dodged his hands and pranced out of reach. He and Giana were yelling, *"Zeus!"*

This was so much fun!

We played the Search game—basically a variation of Stay—all day, until I was so exhausted I plopped my belly into the stream and lapped at the water. It was Work, I realized. I should have figured that out, but sometimes it was hard to tell when we were doing Work and when we were just being happy together.

"Zeus!" Kimo shouted crossly. I heard the distress in his voice, but I had run and run and didn't have the energy to keep doing it. I didn't know what else I could do to please my boy.

At dinner I sprawled under the table. Bear examined me, sniffing my body, probably jealous of the muddy water smells.

"How was training today?" Tutu Nani asked Kimo.

ART #4 TK

Kimo lowered his eyes. "Total fail. He can't learn anything. He *won't*." Kimo gave his father an anguished look. "Would it really have to be for six months, Dad?"

Marco eased back and regarded Kimo carefully. "Tell me what you're doing."

"I say 'Sit,' or 'Drop'—stuff he *knows*—and he just runs around barking. Like, he's forgotten everything."

"You sound upset," Marco observed.

"Of course I'm *upset*," Kimo replied agitatedly. "Do you think I want Zeus sent to prison?"

"I think you're overstating things a little, son. It's hardly prison."

"It's *away from here*."

Tutu Nani nodded. "I would not want to leave the islands, either."

"Zeus was insane. The more I yelled at him, the wilder he got."

"Well, then, I think I know the problem," Marco said thoughtfully.

Everyone turned their attention to Marco, so I did too.

"Dogs need to have their commands come to them calmly," Marco continued. "That's why, no matter how angry I am at a dog, I don't let it show. Same with being sad, or upset, or tense. When I take Bear out and give him a command, it's always in the same tone of voice. Always without any passion. He needs the consistency.

If I get angry and I yell at him to come, he'll think that he's in trouble. Then he doesn't want to come to me.

"On the other hand, if I put too much joy into him doing things right, he might start to forget that his behavior should be connected to the command. Sometimes dogs think that going into a sit makes people so happy that they should do so all the time." He gestured down to Bear, and Bear perked up as if expecting a treat to fly through the air. "See how Bear sits when we're at the table? I can't break him of that one. He believes that sitting's being such a good dog that a treat will be coming eventually."

"Oh," Kimo mumbled guiltily. "I've been giving both dogs treats at the table."

"Yeah," Marco conceded with a sheepish grin, "me too. So try this. Don't use any voice commands at all. Just hand signals. It may seem to Zeus like an entirely new set of commands to learn, and he'll calm down, because he needs to focus. That might help."

"Good idea!" Kimo seemed happier. I thumped my tail against the floor a few times. It was as much as I had energy to do.

"Wouldn't Bear be able to continue to work in search and rescue the same way? With hand signals?" Tutu Nani asked.

Marco's smile was tight and sad. "I'm afraid not. When he's on a search and rescue, he doesn't know he should check for a hand signal—normally, I whistle to get his focus. If he can't hear that whistle, he just keeps looking. That's what happened the last time we went out. And I'm not an effective team member if I'm always chasing after Bear, trying to get his attention."

Tutu Nani frowned. "So what happens to Bear?"

Seven

Marco looked pained. "I'm afraid it's time for Bear to retire. He'll stay at home, keep Nani company, I guess."

"Like a pet," Kimo suggested after a moment.

Marco gave him a sharp look. "I get the point you're making, Kimo, but the donations we've gotten means we have more than enough money to take care of Bear for the rest of his days. Understand the difference? I train and *sell* water rescue dogs. It's what I do. We have to go over this again?"

Kimo lowered his eyes. "No, sir," he told Marco.

There was a silence. Marco shook his head. "I'm sorry, son. I'm upset about Bear, but I shouldn't let that affect how I talk to you. I really do understand how much it bothers you to sell Zeus, but I don't see what I can do. What if you fall in love with the next puppy, and the next? This is probably what it's like to raise canines for seeing-eye training. You treasure the time with them, but you're doing something really, really important—even more important than having a relationship with them."

Kimo responded with a noise so quiet, I wasn't sure Marco heard him.

The next morning Bear and I were both surprised that Marco left without taking any dogs. I made sure Kimo woke up, because Tutu Nani was puttering around in the kitchen, which meant a meal was soon going to be on the table and I didn't want to miss it.

"All right," Kimo groaned at me. "I'm up." We had a breakfast where Kimo was very stingy with any egg sharing. (Tutu Nani fed us a few chunks of what she called *papaya*, which was good but nowhere near as delicious as bacon.) Bear and I followed my boy out into the backyard for more Work.

"Sit!" Bear and I both plunged into a perfect Sit. Cheese treats! Then Kimo held out his hand, palm straight at us, and backed away. I looked to Bear, who was watching alertly, not moving. What was this? I longed to jump out of my Sit and be with my boy, but Bear's intent stare suggested that something was going on, and I had a feeling I should do just what he was doing, even if it didn't make that much sense.

Finally Kimo came running back to us, his mouth in a wide grin. I wagged, seeing the treat before he gave it to me. "Good dogs! Good Stay!" he sang.

That stiff-armed signal became the focus of Work that whole day. For some reason, if I just kept doing Sit and watched him back away, Kimo was happy. And making my boy happy was the most important job I had.

"Bear! You're teaching Zeus what to do!" Kimo praised him. I heard both our names and figured Kimo was saying we were both very good dogs. Which, of course, we were.

Later, Kimo gave the same gesture and called, "Stay!," and I showed Bear I knew that one. I even dashed down and rolled in the stream—best Stay ever! But Bear didn't know enough to follow my example. He kept doing Sit and missed all the fun. Poor Bear.

I guess the big dog felt bad about how that last command had gone, because he was very clingy with Marco every morning after that, giving his person long, mournful looks. "You'll stay with Kimo today, Bear," Marco always told him, on his knees and holding Bear's face in his hands.

"He wants to be with you," Tutu Nani declared softly.

"I know. He'll get used to it eventually, I hope."

"Do you think you'll really need to send Zeus to a trainer in October?" she asked carefully.

Marco stood and drank from his coffee cup. "*Need* to? I don't know. I don't even know if Bonnie can help— Zeus is too full of joy. But having a deadline might be the best thing, get Kimo unstuck." He sighed. "Actually, I'm the one who's stuck, Nani. I have to be consistent with Kimo, be true to my word, so that he knows I always mean what I say. It's one of the most important things a parent can do. It's as true for raising children as it is for dogs. But it's breaking my heart to see my son so attached to Zeus. I guess I didn't realize this would happen. But what else can I do? I just don't feel I have any choice in the matter."

"You're a good father, Marco," Tutu Nani gently assured him.

Bear was devastated whenever Marco kissed him on the head and left. He would lie by the door, staring at it and sighing deeply as though he hoped Marco would hear him and come back. He did seem to perk up when Kimo took us for walks or spent time in the backyard doing the Work thing with us, although I could tell he was still on high alert for Marco to come back.

Every day was pretty much the same, which was how I preferred it. Bear and I were good dogs and did Sit whenever Kimo did his hand gesture, and Kimo showed us a new command, Drop. That meant to put our bellies in the grass and get treats. Sometimes we did Drop and then Kimo would hold out his hand and we had to lie there until he called "Release!," and then treats happened. It was very hard, but I did it because I loved my boy.

And then we had a very loud night, filled with noises and lights in the sky. "Happy Independence Day, Zeus!" Kimo told us.

I ran around the yard, doing Stay.

The morning after the sky got so loud, there was a real excitement coming off my boy.

"Have a good time at day camp," Marco called to Kimo.

"Thanks, Dad!" Kimo answered from down the hall.

"You be a good dog, Bear," Marco said softly as he left.

Bear was crushed yet again. But I was thrilled, because when Kimo finished eating, Tutu Nani took us for a car ride! Bear collapsed into a grumpy heap in his crate, but I was quivering with excitement to sense all the exotic smells flowing past. I stood stiffly, nose up. When we stopped and Giana ran out of a house and jumped into Tutu Nani's truck, I was even more excited.

"Hi, dogs!" she sang out happily.

"You seem jacked for day camp," Kimo observed dryly.

"I remember being *in* day camp when I was little," Giana replied cheerfully. "The counselors and the babysitters seemed so old to me, and now I am one!"

"Not babysitters," Kimo objected. "Interns."

"Sure, if it makes you feel better, though you're going to be watching *babies*."

"What's an intern?" Tutu Nani asked curiously.

"We don't get paid anything," Giana explained. "We just assist the lifeguards, watching the children, which some people would call *babysitting*, when they're in the water. The counselors arrange the activities."

"It's what we have to do to become counselors. Like, training," Kimo added.

"It is a very important job," Tutu Nani suggested. "Taking care of children."

"But in the fall, when day camp moves to weekends, Giana and I will be able to do some activities with the older kids. Like swimming lessons and snorkeling."

"If we don't flunk out as babysitters," Giana commented.

"Interns!" Kimo insisted.

"Camp counselors are paid actual money," Giana continued. "So Kimo can buy his cousin Giana expensive gifts and not just pizza that he eats all of."

Kimo snorted.

"Yes, that's good, but please take seriously the children in your care," Tutu Nani urged. "When they are so little, the waves reach for them."

"Where we'll be, the old fish pond, there's a four-foot wall to keep the waves out. It's like a bathtub, and it's only like two feet at the deepest," Kimo informed her. He turned to Giana. "Bear's helping me train Zeus."

She looked at Bear, so I did too. "What?"

"No lie. Get this: Zeus can *Stay*. Not with a verbal command, but if I do a hand signal and Bear is there, Zeus does what Bear does."

"That's amazing!" Giana grinned.

"We'll do some search and rescue training at the beach before camp starts," Kimo decided. "The book has all these steps, but I think we can mostly skip them as long as Bear is there to demonstrate."

"Skip steps," Giana repeated dubiously.

My nose told me we were headed to the ocean! Soon Tutu Nani stopped her truck and Bear and I were let down onto warm pavement. "'Bye, Tutu," Kimo called, waving as she drove off.

"Okay, what do we do first?" Giana asked.

Kimo reached into his pocket and pulled out a bag that, when opened, flooded the air with what smelled a lot like Tutu Nani's hands when she cooked. "I smeared this tennis ball with fish oil from the skin of the mahi-mahi we ate last night."

"Remind me never to play tennis with you," Giana replied.

"Okay. Let's see if this works. Stay, Bear. Grab Zeus's collar, Giana."

I gathered myself to dash off and do a proper Stay, but Giana thrust her hand out and snagged my collar. I faltered, confused. Why would she stop me from doing what my boy wanted?

Kimo held the ball out for us to sniff. "Okay! Now Scent. Bear, Scent. Zeus, Scent."

I began drooling. Oh, I wanted that ball, with its wonderful smells.

As Kimo walked briskly away, I tracked the scent of that fish ball in his hand. He ducked behind a tree, and then the smell flowed from there as he returned. He held out his marvelously scented fingers. "Okay dogs? Scent!"

Bear and I both gave his hand a powerful sniffing.

"Let Zeus go just after Bear takes off," Kimo requested. "Ready? Bear, Zeus. Search!"

Bear dashed away, and moments later, Giana released her grip. I dashed off behind Bear—he was going after the ball! When he reached the base of the tree, Bear sat and barked and I shoved past him and got my mouth on the ball.

"Zeus! Leave it!" Kimo cried as he ran toward us.

Leave it was a Work command. I didn't think we needed it here at the beach. I took off running, glancing back to make sure Kimo was chasing me.

"Zeus!" he wailed. "Come!"

I had the ball, which had to count for more than all the Work we'd done since I'd joined the family. I dashed around playfully, chewing it, loving the taste.

"Looks like skipping steps really paid off!" Giana called.

I trotted triumphantly up to Giana, showing off, and finally let her snag the ball out of my mouth. "Yuck, Zeus," she complained.

Kimo joined us. "Good first try," he muttered.

Giana laughed, then turned. "The kids are here. Time to get started."

Kimo took my head in his hands. "These are little kids. That means be calm here, Zeus. Okay?"

I whipped my head around because, down at the sandy beach, I saw two little children tottering into the shallow waters.

I was amazed. Basically, they were *puppy humans.* I broke from Kimo and ran down to these little people, play bowing and jumping in the air with joy. I could hear Kimo yelling at me, and he sounded a little cross, so I decided not to go back to him right now. I'd stay with the giggling children.

"Come, Zeus, Come," Kimo called, and he was slapping his legs. I knew what this meant, and after a little bit of hesitation I decided it made more sense to run to him than it did to stay out in the knee-deep water. I scampered up the wet sand and reached him, panting excitedly.

Bear was sticking by Kimo's side, looking up expectantly at my boy. I guessed it was up to me to show him just how a dog has fun at a place like this.

"Zeus, you need to stay with us," Giana told me.

Kimo leaned down and snicked a leash into my collar. "He's, like my dad said, so *rambunctious.*"

I looked up at him, startled. A leash? *Here?*

"Would it be so bad if he just ran around? The kids'll love him."

"He needs to get in control."

Kimo led me over to a tree. It was nice and cool in the shade. "All right," he told me. He left, and I stared at him anxiously, but he soon returned with a bowl of water. I lapped it up just to show that I appreciated the loving gesture, though I wasn't really thirsty. "All right, Drop," he told me. I did Drop, thinking if I did so, he would let me off the leash. "Now you Stay. Stay."

Yes! I *wanted* to do Stay, but first *I had to be let off the leash.*

Bear calmly put his stomach in the grass, patiently watching all the children run around. No matter how many times I showed him, he'd never figured out how to do Stay.

Kimo walked away, and I twisted and turned and pulled at the very end of that leash, frantic to be closer to my boy. I watched as he and Giana paced back and forth on the beach. Every now and then they waded in to grab a child who seemed to be having trouble standing upright in the shallow water. There were other adult humans there as well, and they were talking to older children and forming groups to play games.

This would have been the most fun day of my life if I hadn't been tied to the stupid tree. How could Kimo have forgotten me like this? Since I couldn't pull the leash loose and I couldn't twist out of my collar, I tried whining. It didn't help at all. Finally I gave up and took a nap.

Bear and I were both dozing when the air was suddenly split with the shrill cries of children shrieking. A big wave had smashed over the top of the rock wall, and the resulting ripples had knocked over several small children.

Bear was instantly on his feet, dashing for the water.

Eight

As soon as the children fell over, Giana and Kimo ran to them, pulling them upright and setting them on their feet. Bear hit the water moments later. I noticed him bounding over to a small child who was swimming facedown. He gripped the little girl by the back of the jacket she wore and lifted her all the way out of the water, so that she was dangling and dripping.

"Good dog," I heard Kimo praise Bear, as he gently took the girl from the big dog's jaws.

I was being a good dog too, I thought. I could have run out there in the pond to play, but I was still tied to a tree.

I noticed a few of the other humans had dashed out to help, and now they were all anxiously checking the children, making sure they hadn't missed anyone.

"Bear. Such a good dog." Kimo blew out a breath. "Well, that was . . . exciting."

"That was *amazing*," Giana corrected. "Did your dad teach Bear that?"

Kimo shrugged. "Bear's used to all sorts of situations. He's been trained to recognize when people are in trouble in the water. I guess he just did what he thought made the most sense." Kimo gave Bear a treat, which was very unfair. I could be doing Work and getting treats if only Kimo would let me.

"When the kids leave today, let's grab the mouth-to-mouth training dummy—the child-sized one—and see if Bear can do it again," Giana suggested. She led Bear back up and told him to Drop near me. Then she told him to Stay, which he still didn't know how to do.

I regarded him curiously. The wistful, sad dog who always watched so miserably when Marco left in the morning had been replaced by an alert, watchful dog who was even more focused on the playing children than he had been before. I wondered what had changed.

After all the children left, Giana brought out a doll from a big wooden box.

"Okay," Giana announced, struggling to put a puffy jacket on the doll. "This is the same size as the other kids we're babysitting—I mean *interning*." Giana carried the doll out into the pond and threw it into the water, facedown. "*Bear!*" she cried shrilly.

Bear instantly broke from his place next to me on the beach and plunged into the water, kicking up spray. He lunged through the shallows, reached the doll, grabbed it with his mouth, and pulled it up in the air. Giana applauded.

"Really good dog, Bear!" Kimo called.

I sat down in disgust. They had forgotten all about me. I watched Giana do Work with Bear in the water, throwing the doll down and letting him pick it up over and over again. Kimo came to me and told me I was a good dog, for no reason, and fed me a treat. I was just sitting there and I was getting treats for that. Life wasn't making any sort of sense.

I was glad when they seemed to remember who the best dog was and let me off the leash at last. We did more Work called Search. First there was the stiff palm, meaning "Don't move." Kimo then said, "Stay," so I gave it my best, leaping and running and showing Bear what to do.

"I'm giving up on that for now," Kimo told Giana. "I'll get back to it once he's calmed."

Over and over, Giana would hold out a sleeve for me to sniff, saying, "Scent!," then run away. Bear and I watched this impassively, but when Kimo commanded, "Search!," we gleefully ran to Giana and jumped on her.

Well, *I* jumped on her, anyway. Bear just wasn't that kind of dog.

Since Tutu Nani had taken us to the beach, I expected Tutu Nani to come fetch us, but instead it was Marco in his Jeep. Bear and I were in the far back, in our respective crates, but we could still hear the people very clearly, and I listened closely for mentions of cheese.

ART #5 TK

"How's the training? Did I give you two enough extra time before coming to pick you up?" Marco wanted to know.

Kimo sighed. "Plenty of time, but Zeus doesn't get *anything*. I gave him like thirty treats today."

Marco nodded. "Labradors are easy to train because they're so food oriented. But if you're feeling stuck, another way to do it is to try play."

"Play?"

"As a reward."

There was a silence. "We're not going to have to send Zeus to the lady in California in October, Dad," Kimo announced with finality. "He's a smart dog. He'll get this." He wasn't looking at Marco—his eyes were staring straight ahead. "Sometimes plans change."

Marco glanced at Kimo. "I'm not as inflexible as you think, son. I'm just trying to do my best here. If you teach Zeus the basics and, most importantly, get him to calm down, I'll cancel his trip to Bonnie's in October."

School was long forgotten in favor of day camp. I didn't mind at all. Even though I spent way too much time sitting under a tree, day camp always started and ended by games of Work.

The days we didn't do day camp, we would go out into the backyard. Bear was happy when this happened, even though "happy" for Bear was nowhere near the thrilling joy I felt when I was doing . . . well, anything. But Bear liked being told what to do, and I did too, even though I did things my own way. Work made me feel like I was doing something important, and pleasing my boy too. I had a sense of purpose whenever we did Work.

One morning Kimo walked with Bear and me out to the backyard and announced, "Bear. Speak!"

I jumped when Bear unexpectedly barked. Then Kimo gave him a treat, because that was just the sort of day it was going to be. "Zeus, Speak!"

I watched. "Bear. Speak!"

Bear barked. And got a treat.

I lay down, doing Drop on my own, bored with the whole thing. I wasn't particularly hungry.

Kimo regarded me for a time, and then he pulled out an old, floppy sock and fed a ball into it.

I stared in amazement. My boy was combining two of the best toys ever invented, a ball and a sock! I couldn't imagine anything more wonderful. I could already feel this new thing in my mouth as Kimo held it out in front of him, and I eagerly lunged for it.

"No. Drop," Kimo told me.

I did Drop, but I didn't understand. When Kimo commanded, "Stay," and held up his palm, I lunged for the new toy. "Oh, Zeus," he sighed.

We did this strange new Work over and over again. He said, "Stay," backing up, his palm held stiffly in front of him. What did he want me to do—run around for Stay or be still for the held-out palm? I watched him for a moment and then ran to him, trying to make him happy, grabbing at the ball-in-a-sock toy dangling from his back pocket.

He didn't like that. We returned to the original spot and I did Sit.

Bear had been watching all this, and I could tell he wanted that sock toy, but whenever Kimo said, "Stay," Bear would freeze in place, giving me first shot at it.

Tutu Nani came out to watch me outsmart Bear. Kimo gave her a sad smile. "I'm not doing very well," he lamented to her.

"You are very loving and patient with Zeus," Tutu Nani observed. "That's what's most important, Kimo. The rest will come, in time."

"I don't actually have much time," Kimo reminded her. "Dad gave me until October. That's like two months. Giana and I have been training Zeus all summer, but at the rate I'm going, when October comes, Zeus will still know *nothing*."

"What if you let Bear show Zeus what to do, just like you told us in the car?"

Later we did another Work called Heel. Bear was off leash, and he seemed content not to pursue excellent scents all around us. Instead, he just kept close to Kimo's side.

I was thrilled to be on a walk and I ran around and around, tangling the leash, teaching Kimo he should remove it so I could have even more fun. Bear remained focused and dour. I liked Bear, but he was no substitute for a sock, especially one with a ball in it.

There was Work in the backyard and Work on the beach before day camp. So much Work! I'd come to love it. And I was learning so many things.

Speak meant "Bark and run around." *Scent* meant "Smell this, then jump on it and try to grab it!" *Search* was a little more difficult, because it could mean "Run to Giana" or "Find the fishy ball" or "Look for the ball-in-a-sock." Even more confusing, once I did Search, I was told to then do Sit and do Speak, which made no sense to me. Much more fun to do Stay, running around, jumping at Bear, rolling in the sand.

"He's not getting it," Kimo moaned.

"Let's just keep trying," Giana encouraged him.

I was doing Bear a real favor, showing him what a dog needs to understand, but in the backyard he always had one eye out for Marco coming home. And on the beach, when the children were there, he just sat and watched, day after day. Poor Bear.

What I was doing—Work—was important, extremely so, to Kimo and Giana. It gave me purpose, which made me even happier than doing Stay the way it should be done.

I even stopped being bothered when I was leashed to a tree at day camp. Doing Work in the morning tired me so much that all I wanted to do was nap in the shade, anyway.

"You know what would be fun?" Giana asked as we sat near the parking lot toward the end of the day, waiting for either Tutu Nani or Marco to decide to come get us. "Teaching the dogs to surf."

Kimo stared at her. "To surf. For fun."

"Right, it would be fun," Giana repeated, looking at Kimo in confusion. "Don't you think so?"

"Do you know what today is? It's August twentieth. School starts soon, and Zeus can't Heel, doesn't really do Speak—at least, once he starts, he doesn't *stop*—and he's way, way far from learning how to stay."

"He does know how to stay," Giana replied reasonably. "And he did it. Like, once."

"Exactly."

"He knows what it means, he just doesn't like to do it."

"It's like my dad said, he's too wild. He's going to have to go to boot camp or whatever and I can't do anything about it."

"I know it's important, Kimo. But it's like you're a full-time dog trainer, now. It's all you want to do. It's the end of summer. We should be having fun!"

Kimo's face was unhappy, so I licked it.

At day camp the next day, just as my senses were telling me it was about time for the children to leave and for us to do Work, another big wave came sweeping over the wall, knocking the children over. Bear reacted instantly, and moments later stood holding a little dripping girl in his jaws.

I glanced at a woman who was striding down the

sand, her hands on her hips. She marched straight up to Kimo as he pulled the girl from Bear's mouth.

"Your dog just attacked my child!" she shouted angrily.

"No, ma'am," Kimo replied firmly, but politely. "Bear is a trained water rescue dog. When he saw your little girl fall over, he reacted instinctively."

Giana nodded.

"Dogs," the woman continued in a stern tone, "are not allowed on the beach. They're supposed to stay up in the trees."

"Normally, yes, ma'am," Kimo agreed. "But this was an emergency, at least to Bear, and he reacted the way we would all want him to."

"You're wrong," the woman snapped. "You should be fired."

"Fired? For watching over your child while you texted somebody on your phone?" Giana challenged her. "Can you imagine what would have happened if your little girl had to rely on *you*?"

The woman aimed a scorching look at Giana. "This doesn't concern you." She reached down and snatched up her daughter and marched away. The daughter, looking over her shoulder, gave a tiny wave at Kimo, Giana, and Bear, but not me.

Then the woman turned and pointed a finger. "This isn't over," she shouted. "I promise you!"

Nine

I thought it was completely unnecessary, but people started saying "school" again. Worse, everyone started *doing* school again.

I didn't understand why we couldn't just keep going to day camp, but the mornings had changed. My boy woke up earlier, groaning when Marco proclaimed, "It's 6:52," and then he was gone. Tutu Nani cuddled with me and Bear, who was also depressed, but it just wasn't the same as having Kimo's arms around me.

Bear's mood turned very bleak, but after he came back from doing school, Kimo would do Work with us, repeating, over and over, the games we'd learned. I loved Scent and Search, and I slowly learned that at the end of Search I would be rewarded if I did Sit and Speak. I also figured out that there was far more freedom with Heel if I clung to Kimo's side and walked, because whenever I dashed to the end of the leash Kimo would halt and we'd hold in a Sit until I wanted to bark in frustration.

And then there was Stay. Something very bad had happened: Stay, I'd come to realize, no longer meant Stay. It meant Drop and hold still until Kimo called, "Release!"

"Watch this," Kimo told Giana, several days after he'd reintroduced the dreaded concept of school into our lives. We had walked up the muddy trail and were at the top, where a thin stream of water cascaded from high up the rocks and splashed into a delightfully cool pool. It was the birthplace of the stream behind our house. "Zeus?"

Bear and I perked up. This felt like Work.

Kimo pointed at the ground. "Drop."

I put my stomach in the delightful mud, as did Bear.

"Zeus? Bear? Stay! Stay!" Kimo held out a stiff hand.

He and Giana turned away, heading back up the hill. Giana kept turning to look at me, and I'd tense, but no one said anything.

I glanced at Bear when the humans vanished over the crest of the hill. The only sound was the constant shower of water spilling from the high rocks. Bear watched the place where we'd last seen the people, not moving.

It was agony, but this was the nature of Work, overcoming being a normal dog to being a dog with purpose.

Finally I heard a call from far away. "Bear! Zeus! Come!"

At last! I broke out of Sit, but Bear didn't move. I'd been summoned with "Come!," but now I hesitated. I didn't want to leave my best dog friend behind.

I stared at him, then turned and looked pointedly in the direction where our people had vanished.

"Come!" Kimo called again.

I got right in Bear's face and barked—what else could I do? Bear was startled. Clearly, something unusual was happening. When I turned and began slowly trotting after Kimo and Giana, he seemed to understand.

And I understood something new, too. When the people were out of view, when we couldn't see them but could only smell and hear them, it was my job to show Bear what to do.

The rest of the time, Bear would demonstrate and I would copy his behavior and get a treat. But this was the opposite, and Bear got it at last. He dashed after me as I scrambled up the hill.

Giana and Kimo were sitting at a wooden table. Kimo handed us both treats, and Bear gave me a grateful glance. His instinct to mimic me had led to peanut butter, which I loved as much as chicken. But not bacon!

Giana laughed delightedly. "Zeus! You can *stay*!" She beamed at Kimo. "It's not even the first of September. What happened? How did you do it?"

Kimo was grinning. "Honestly? I think Bear did it. Zeus got tired of Bear getting all the fun and all the treats for Stay."

"All the search and rescue work you've been doing really does give Zeus focus," Giana told him. "He's become so much less crazy."

"That's not the only reason I'm doing it," Kimo told her.

Giana's eyes crinkled. "Oh, you think maybe I don't get it?"

"Get what?"

"Bear's retired. And your dad has said it—when there's a lost hiker, a dog can cover ten times the ground that a person can. You think if you train Zeus to be search and rescue, your dad will want him on the squad. To replace Bear."

Kimo looked away. "I get that it's a dumb idea."

Giana smiled. "I'm in."

He blinked at her.

She nodded. "It's not a dumb idea at all. I think it makes all the sense in the world. We'll train Zeus and your dad will let Zeus replace Bear. Perfect. Only you're missing the bigger picture."

Kimo cocked his head. "What do you mean?"

"Uncle Marco is always saying it: Bear can do everything except handle the helicopters." "So . . ."

"So we need to train Zeus in water rescue, too," Kimo finished for her.

She nodded. "By the end of October, Zeus has to be just like Bear in every way, except with better hearing."

"Yeah. Yeah! Dad will see Zeus as Bear's logical

replacement. And I won't tell him about it yet—not until Zeus is perfect."

"I so understand it now that you've said the exact same thing back to me!" Giana laughed. "Before you explained to me what just I told you, I was completely ignorant."

"Sure, ha-ha."

Bear and I were hearing our names a lot, but there were no more peanut butter treats.

"Okay, so, how do we start?" Kimo wanted to know.

"We go surfing."

"Surfing," my boy repeated doubtfully.

Giana laughed again. "You should see your face. Look, I get how important Zeus is to you. And we've got a plan. So can you maybe relax a little? You're so serious, just like your dad. Let's take the dogs out and *play*. Remind them that water is fun. We can figure out the rescue part some other day. It's Sunday tomorrow, and until day camp weekends fire up, it's our day off! A lot of people—you probably don't know this—use their days off to *take a day off*."

The next morning, Bear and I rode in Tutu Nani's truck. We didn't go to the flat pool but to a different beach, where the waves were louder and there were no children in the water.

I was excited and kept glancing at Bear. As usual, he couldn't be bothered to change his expression or even pick up his ears. I wondered if it was my purpose to teach Bear how to be a dog.

Kimo unloaded two long, shiny boards from the back of the truck.

"You two have fun," Tutu Nani said with a smile. She focused on Kimo. "Especially you, Kimo. Not every day can be about training dogs."

"That's what I keep telling him!" Giana replied.

Kimo looked weary. "Okay, I get it."

Tutu Nani's truck made a beeping noise as she drove away. My boy put the boards flat on the sand. "Okay." He patted a board. "Climb on. Let's go."

I looked up questioningly, and then was surprised when Kimo picked me up and placed me on the board. Instantly, I jumped off. The board was slippery, difficult to stand on. It reminded me a little of the slide down which I'd plummeted the day I met Bear and Marco.

Kimo reached down for me again. "Zeus," he told me patiently, "you need to Stay." There was that word again!

Kim sat me on the board. For a moment I nearly did real Stay, fun Stay. But then I realized this was the new, motionless Stay he was talking about.

I would never understand why Kimo liked the second version of Stay so much.

The board carried the strong smell of ocean, and also of Kimo's feet. Every time I tried to get off, Kimo would shake his head and put me back on. Meanwhile, Bear climbed up on Giana's board and stood there, glumly watching what was happening. Giana gave him a treat.

I thought about it. If treats were to be given for merely standing on a flat slide, I wasn't going to question it.

"All right, he's got the first step," Kimo announced, after I finally got my own cheesy treat. "Now watch this."

Kimo surprised me by jumping on the board with me. Immediately it began to shift beneath my feet. He walked back and forth on it and I splayed my claws wide to stay on, trying to find purchase on the smooth surface, doing Stay.

When my back legs slipped off, Kimo waited while I scrambled back on, then he gave me a treat. He jumped up and down and I clung to the board and got a treat. I noticed that once I got used to the idea that the board was going to move around, I could hang on. And hang on I did—receiving treats each time.

"All right!" Giana sang with a happy smile. "Bear, you ready to show Zeus how to surf?" She glanced over at Kimo. "When was the last time Bear went?"

"I took him out a few times before spring break."

"This is going to be so much fun!"

I was completely unprepared for what happened next. First, Kimo let me get off the wobbly board. He put me in an entirely new sort of harness, a puffy jacket with a handle on the back where a leash would usually go. I figured it was probably the same as the harness Kimo put on Bear. Then, calling me, Kimo picked up his board and held it over his head.

Giana grabbed hers and carried it the same way. We followed, Bear and I, as they strode through the sand and down to where the water was lapping at the shore.

Bear didn't hesitate and neither did I. Swimming with my boy was the most fun I could possibly imagine, and I thought Bear probably felt the same.

What puzzled me, though, was that right about when the water was halfway to Giana's knees, Bear threw himself onto her board. He shook to get some of the water out of his fur and balanced there, and Giana didn't break step. She just kept dragging her board out into the waves.

"You can do it," Kimo told me. Grinning, he reached down and scooped me up with one arm and set me on his board.

It was even more wobbly in the water than it had been on the sand. Kimo moved to the back and pushed down on the board so that when each wave came in, the moving water punched the board but didn't sweep over the top of it.

BAM! The next wave knocked the front end of the board up. It tilted, and I fell off. What were we doing?

Giana, I noticed, was lying flat on her board, and so was Bear.

Kimo hauled me out of the water and placed me back

ART #6 TK

on the board. A wave came—*BAM!*—and knocked me off.

Why on earth didn't we just go back to shore? The board had been slippery there, but it didn't bounce around like this.

I fell off with every wave until I understood that if I just mimicked Bear and lay flat, taking the shock with my whole body, I could remain on the board. "Good dog, Zeus!"

I panted with excitement that we were doing whatever we were doing.

Kimo still had soggy treats in his pocket. I could smell them, but there was no treat necessary right now because I was with my boy out in the water, and that was the best reward of all.

The swells lifted and dropped the board beneath me. Sometimes it was a little too much and I fell off and swam immediately to Kimo, who put me back up, climbing up behind me.

A larger wave was gathering strength out in the ocean. I could hear it coming. Kimo spun the board around so now I was looking at the beach. I glanced over and saw that Giana had done the same thing with Bear. The board was surging ahead and she was standing right behind him!

"This is it, Zeus! Are you ready?" Kimo called.

Ten

The back end of the board rose and the front end dropped and I knew what this was—a slide! I got ready for water to spray my eyes. I began to slip forward, just as I'd done with Marco all those weeks ago, but Kimo grabbed the handle on my harness, yanking me into the center of the board, and now we were *moving*!

I felt as if I was falling, but I wasn't. The wave kept pace with us, somehow. Bear, I noticed, remained standing in front of Giana, who was cheering and clutching his handle. We washed rapidly toward the beach, and then Giana and Kimo slipped into the water. Bear leaped into the foam, so I did too. Swimming!

It was Work, because we did it again and again. Every time I started to fall, Kimo held me up. With each try, I felt more comfortable, more stable. "Good dog!" Kimo shouted joyously. "You're surfing, Zeus! You're a surf dog. A surf dog."

Surf dog sounded a bit like *good dog.* That was nice.

We were out floating, bobbing in the waves, when Kimo leaned over and frowned. "Some haole threw a beer can over the side. See it down there?"

Giana nodded. "Think you can dive down to it?"

"Oh yeah."

I stared, startled, when Kimo dropped his head and plunged off the board into the water. He took a couple of deep breaths and vanished. The last thing I saw were his feet.

Bear was watching impassively, but I was frantic. My boy had just fallen into the water and disappeared!

I could no longer see him, but his scent was bubbling up from beneath the waves. Without hesitation, my nails scrabbling, I plunged off the board and dove, following my nose. I had to save my boy!

Finally, I could see enough of him to put my mouth softly on his arm, right where it joined his shoulder. Startled, he whipped his head around, but when I aimed for the surface, I could feel him kicking alongside me, and we rose together.

When our heads broke through, Kimo was laughing. "Zeus just did water rescue! He's a natural at it!"

Both my boy and Giana were so happy that I hoped I'd be a surf dog every day.

But the next time Tutu Nani drove us to the ocean, we were back at day camp. We were doing Scent and Search while waiting for the children to arrive, when a man walked up the beach toward us. His skin and hair were the color of Kimo's, and he smelled like the sun and the ocean. "Hey, Kimo. Hi, Giana."

"Aloha, Mikoa."

He reached down and petted Bear, so I stood and shook myself expectantly, ready for my turn. "So . . . is this the criminal?"

Kimo winced.

"That's Bear," Giana told him sunnily. "He made a mom feel bad she wasn't paying attention when her child got knocked over and nearly killed by a wave."

"Sure," the man agreed affably. "Though that is sort of what *you* guys are here for."

"Oh, we ran out too," Kimo assured him quickly, "but Bear got to this one girl and lifted her clear out of the water."

There was an awkward silence before the stranger spoke again. "So, thing is, the woman sort of demanded we fire you, Kimo."

Giana's mouth opened, and Kimo stared at the man. Bear and I watched him carefully. My boy seemed upset, and this man might be the reason. I'd better keep an eye on him.

The man held up a hand. "But I told her that's not my decision. I told her that's the head lifeguard's call—

Noa Iona. And he's attending a class in Oregon. So I'd say nothing's going to happen until he returns—but maybe leave the dogs at home from now on?"

Giana shook her head. "That's not fair, Mikoa. She's lying about what happened. We should ban *her* from the beach."

Kimo nodded. "Sure, we can leave Bear, but I'm working with Zeus, trying to teach him to be calm, so I'd like to keep bringing him. I leave him tied up here in the trees, so there shouldn't be a problem."

"No problem I can see," the man confirmed with a grin. "Like I said, not my decision one way or another. But the lady did threaten to call the mayor's office."

"Sorry, Bear," Giana said sadly.

Bear and I wagged, hoping to cheer everybody up.

Later on, Marco's Jeep picked us up. "How was it today?" he asked.

"We ran into some major stupidity," Giana replied hotly. "And now we're *fired*."

"What?"

"Actually," Kimo corrected more calmly, "that's not exactly it. See, Giana got the idea to train Bear to help rescue kids who have fallen over in the pond. Sometimes a big wave will breach the wall. When that happens, the kids usually all go down at once, and some of the younger ones can't seem to get back up. Bear runs to them and picks them up by the life jacket."

Marco was grinning as he nodded.

"Then a lady was upset because we interrupted her texting," Giana put in.

"Oh?"

Kimo nodded. "She got really angry when Bear pulled her girl out of the water. So we're not allowed to bring him back."

Marco's grin faded. "All right. I know there are a lot of people your age competing for the intern positions, so I don't want you to get in even the tiniest bit of trouble. Interns have an inside track for camp counselor, and they usually pick lifeguards from the counselors. We didn't have interns when I was your age, but I was a counselor before lifeguarding."

"I'm amazed!" Giana exclaimed.

Marco seemed a little puzzled. "That I was a counselor?"

"That you were ever our age!"

Marco laughed.

Kimo held up a hand, but there were no treats in it. He began pointing, one by one, to his fingers. "Counselor, to lifeguard, to Search and Rescue, to EMT, to paramedic, to dog trainer of rescue canines."

"That was the plan," Marco agreed.

"That's my plan, too," Kimo said seriously.

Marco started in surprise. "You never told me that."

"I want to do what you do, Dad," Kimo told him.

Marco swallowed. "That means the world to me, son," he murmured, his voice rough. "But I won't take it as a promise. As Giana points out all the time, plans change. I just want what's best for you, no matter what that is, or where it takes you."

"I know that, Dad," Kimo said in a similarly hoarse voice.

Giana was smiling, so I wagged. Finally Marco cleared his throat. "Let's leave Bear at home. He can keep your Tutu company."

"That's not fair to Bear," Giana objected.

Marco shrugged. "It is what it is."

"Well, it should be what it *isn't*," she retorted, frowning. That earned her a grin from Kimo.

The next morning Bear watched a little forlornly as Kimo loaded me into my crate in Tutu Nani's truck. We drove to the ocean, to day camp, but the Work before the children arrived was completely different than it had ever been.

Instead of hunting for Giana or socks or shoes or balls, Kimo put the same bulky vest on me that I'd worn when I was a surf dog. Then he sat with me on the sand while Giana swam out beyond the rock wall, where the waves surged. I watched suspiciously as Giana paddled away from us in the currents.

"What's Giana doing?" Kimo asked me. His tone of voice made me think he was about to tell me to do

Search and to find Giana, wherever she was hiding—but there was no place for her to hide out here.

Giana started waving her arms. "Rescue, Zeus!" Kimo told me urgently.

I jumped and barked. I didn't know what Rescue meant, but it sounded exciting.

Kimo raced into the waves, and I followed. I'd been right! Rescue was fun!

We swam to Giana, the waves tossing us. When we reached her, Kimo called, "Okay, Zeus, Circle! Circle!" He swam behind her.

Another new word? This was utter baffling, so I followed my boy. We went around Giana a few times, Kimo calling, "Circle!," and then we all headed for shore and he gave me a treat.

Then we did the same thing again. That's how I knew I was doing Work. Repetition meant Kimo wanted me to learn something, even if I wasn't in the mood.

The children came and I was tied to a tree again. I missed Bear. People decide which dogs stay home and which ones are tied to trees at the beach, but that doesn't mean dogs like it.

In fact, Bear *hated* it. I could tell by his reaction when I greeted him after Tutu Nani drove us home. He was gloomy, even for him. Only when Marco walked in the door did he seem anything near normal.

When Kimo did school, I would lie with Bear in the

yard, sharing his discontent. Eventually he'd agree to play with me for a while, which would cheer both of us up, but we really were just waiting and waiting for our people to come home.

Work became both more complicated and more fun over the next several days. I learned a new way to do Search. It involved many balls, which bounced out of a box and rolled all over the floor, making me quiver with the desire to chase them all down.

"Stay," Kimo warned me. I knew what that meant, so, though I was very tense, I held still. He had several balls clutched in his hands, but he thrust my favorite, the fish-smelling ball, at my nose. "Scent!" he commanded me.

Then Kimo walked briskly away from me and tossed balls to the left, the right, in front of him . . . everywhere! It was all I could do to remain on Stay. "Good dog," Giana murmured from behind me.

When Kimo returned, he held out his hand and it was rich with the magnificent fish scent. "Scent, Zeus. Scent. Ready? Okay, Search, Zeus. Search," he told me.

I ran out and grabbed the first ball I found and brought it back to him, wagging.

"Thank you," Kimo told me. He gave me a treat! "Zeus, Search!"

I ran out and fetched another ball. Again, a treat! I glanced at Giana, who was nodding encouragement.

When I came across the ball with the amazing odors, Kimo gave me a whole *handful* of treats. And he let me play with a ball-in-a-sock!

After a while, I learned that all balls are wonderful, there was something very special about the fish ball, so the next time Kimo said, "Scent," and let me sniff fish and then threw the balls and said, "Search!," I ran straight toward where my nose led me and brought back the pungent ball first. I was right! Kimo gave me treats and let me tug on the sock.

"He figured that out fast!" Giana said happily.

So that was the new Scent and Search. It had changed, the way Stay changed, but that was, I now understood, the nature of Work.

The next day of day camp, I saw Bear watching from the front window as we left. Even without being able to smell him, I could tell how sad he was to be abandoned. First Marco had left without him, and now *we* were doing the same thing.

As we sat in the car, I whined just a little, to tell Kimo that Bear was alone and that something should be done about it.

"I know, Zeus." Kimo rubbed behind my ears, which did make me feel better. "It's not fair. But we can't change it right now."

And we drove to the beach, leaving Bear by himself.

For Work before the children arrived, we had a

bunch of balls, again! That made me so excited I forgot about Bear for the moment.

Giana picked one ball up and squirted something on it, a flowery spray so strong my nose crinkled. She held the ball out to me and I looked away from it, my eyes watering. I watched her toss several balls onto the sand and into the trees, easily able to track the one she'd perfumed. When she returned, I reluctantly sniffed her outstretched palm. "Scent!" Yes, it was overwhelmingly coated with the same stench.

Kimo was grinning. "Okay, Zeus, you ready?"

I heard the question in his voice and glanced at the box of balls. The fishy one was in there, with a couple others.

"Zeus . . . Search!"

I took a step toward the box with the fishy ball in it. Then I hesitated.

Usually Search was finding the wonderful fishy ball. But something was different today, wasn't it? Giana's hand had that awful smell. And she was the one who'd said to do Search. Not Kimo.

I trotted away hesitantly. Then I paused and looked over my shoulder at my boy. "Good dog!" he encouraged.

It seemed I was doing Search right, even though that mean walking away from the fishy ball.

The flowery ball was easy to find. It tasted as bad as

it smelled, but Giana and Kimo were so ecstatic when I grabbed it that I put up with the wretched sting on my tongue until I spat the ball out at Giana's feet. She was welcome to it.

"I have to say it, Kimo, you're really good at dog training," Giana told my boy. "You're bad at everything else, but you're amazing with Zeus."

"Thank you, dear cousin."

"Hard to believe that it'll be Halloween soon."

"I know."

Giana turned serious eyes on Kimo. "You're cutting it pretty close, don't you think? You need to show your dad that Zeus has calmed down and mastered all the basics before he ships him to what's-her-name in California."

Kimo nodded slowly.

"What's wrong?"

I sensed my boy's distress as he met Giana's gaze. "What if Zeus fails?" he asked softly.

Eleven

K imo!" Giana snapped.

Kimo started in surprise.

"You need to pull yourself out of it," Giana said firmly. "I told you that you're really good at dog training. Watch. Zeus! Sit! Drop!"

I did as Giana told me.

"Speak!"

I barked.

"Stay!" Giana commanded. "Come on, Kimo."

I watched in distress as they walked into the trees. After a time, I couldn't see them and I could hardly smell them at all—they were just trace scents on the wind.

It felt like school, they were gone so long.

When finally I saw them coming, my tail thrashed the sandy soil, but I remained in Drop and Stay until Kimo called, "Release!" Then I closed the distance to him, sobbing with relief.

"See?" Giana said triumphantly. "I was right. At this one thing, you're an idiot savant. On all other things, you're just an idiot."

They grinned at each other. Kimo gave me a fishy treat. He was much happier now, of course, because I was finally next to him, where I belonged.

"All right," he decided. "It's time to tell my dad."

That afternoon, after the children left day camp, we did the Work where Giana swam out and waved her arms and Kimo and I swam to her after he said, "Rescue!" Kimo had gotten into the habit of grabbing the handle on the puffy vest he had me wear, and swimming was more difficult because he was lazier and lazier each time. I had to drag more and more of his weight to do Circle, which meant to swim just out of arm's reach of Giana while she and Kimo talked.

"Did you know there's a dog surfing contest every July? We should enter next year!" Giana told Kimo, as a wave lifted all of us.

"Okay, except we're not dogs."

"Ha-ha."

"Good dog, Zeus. Go in!" Kimo commanded me. This meant I should swim to shore, with Giana holding the handle and Kimo swimming next to me.

"I mean, the dogs surf by *themselves*. I was thinking, what if we got both Bear and Zeus on a surfboard together? They'd win the contest for sure!" Giana enthused, while I paddled hard, pulling her weight.

"Neither one can surf by themselves. What makes you think they can do it together?"

"I taught *you* to surf, didn't I? The dogs should be easier—they're smarter."

We were approaching shore, and I appreciated that the waves were doing their best to thrust me forward, because it was tiring to drag Giana through the water.

"Good dog, Zeus!" Kimo praised. We played tug on a ball-in-a-sock, and then Giana swam back out, because this was Work and that's what we did, over and over again.

When we got home, Bear was lying in the shade in the backyard and didn't lift his head until I licked his snout. Then he gave me a disgusted look. He had no energy, no joy, nothing but weariness.

He perked up, though, when Kimo produced a bouncy ball. I wouldn't even want to meet a dog who wasn't excited by the sight of a ball in a person's hand.

Kimo and Giana were still throwing balls for Bear and me in the driveway when Marco's Jeep pulled in. Bear went to him, wagging and whimpering, and Marco knelt and gave Bear love, so I went over and jumped on both of them.

"Take it easy, Zeus," Marco warned. He pushed me off of him, which was silly. Weren't we all happy to see each other? I was so delighted that I snatched up a ball and raced in a circle around the yard, swerving to be close to Bear each time so he'd see that I had a ball and that he needed to chase me to take it.

"Hi, Dad," Kimo greeted.

"Aloha, Uncle Marco," Giana added.

Bear was still focused on Marco, not me and my marvelous tennis ball. I danced closer to him, shaking my head, and bumped into Marco's leg. He staggered sideways.

"So, Dad. You ready to see how Zeus does with Stay?" Kimo asked.

Marco eyed me. I turned my head up to him and wagged very hard. Maybe he'd like to chase me and try to get the ball away from me, since Bear was being so dull?

"Okay, son. Show me," Marco agreed.

We passed through the house and out into the back-yard. For some reason, Kimo seemed tense.

"You ready? Zeus, you ready?" Kimo held out the ball-in-a-sock. I spit out the ball I already had in my mouth and I stared at this, the best toy in the world, wanting it so badly that everything else was forgotten.

Kimo held out a stiff palm. "Stay, Zeus. Stay."

That. I froze, and Bear did too. Kimo shook the ball-in-a-sock as he backed up. Oh, I didn't want Bear to get that sock, but after all the Work I'd done, I understood that if I waited, Kimo would give it to me.

Finally, *finally*, he yelled, "Zeus, Come!," and I ran to him, and he threw the sock and I chased it and pounced on it and grabbed it and shook it as hard as I could

Bear didn't move until Kimo very loudly called, "Bear, Come." And then we all returned to Marco's side. Kimo was grinning. "See? What do you think?"

Marco nodded. "Very nice," he replied faintly.

Kimo looked puzzled. "What's wrong? We beat the deadline! And he does a pretty good Heel, and Drop, and Speak, too. You don't have to send him to California."

"He's calm, too," Giana added eagerly. "At day camp, we tell him to Drop and Stay, and then it doesn't matter what happens. The kids can run right past his nose, but he just waits."

"It's everything you asked for," Kimo finished up.

Macro drew in a deep breath. His face was troubled. "Kimo. Something happened."

Kimo and Giana glanced at each other. "What do you mean?"

"Look, first I want to say I'm really proud at how much work you've done with Zeus. I honestly thought, the first time I tried to get him to stay, that he would never be anything but a berserk puppy. It's testimony to your efforts. And he does seem a bit more calm. But, well . . . I still think he's too high-strung to be in water rescue. That can be a problem with this breed. For water rescue, you don't just need a dog who can follow basic commands. He needs to be calm and steady in very tense situations. I've thought it over very carefully and I've made a decision. I'm not going to go on with formal rescue training for Zeus. I just don't think he's going to work out."

"He's already—" Kimo started to say.

Giana chopped the air with the edge of her hand to cut him off. "You said something happened," she prompted impatiently.

"Right." Marco gave Kimo a level look. "Last week I got a call. The shelter where I adopted Zeus has a pregnant Newfoundland who was just surrendered. You've heard me say Newfies are excellent at water rescue—they love the ocean, they're big, and they're calm. Bear's part Newfie. You've been saying Zeus is more of a pet than a working dog, and I agree. I know you're not going to like this, but I want to return Zeus and get one of the new pups."

Kimo gasped. Marco held up his hand, so both Bear and I did Sit and Stay. "Hear me out, Kimo. It's not as bad as you think. Zeus won't be auctioned off to somebody on the mainland or anything like that. Instead, he'll be adopted by someone on the island—*this* island. You'll still get to see him. And I promise to keep you involved in the training of the Newfie. You're good—no, you're *excellent*—at this."

I felt the distress pouring off my boy and broke Stay to nuzzle his hand to remind him his dog was here to help with whatever was going on. "When?" Kimo whispered.

"When . . . ? Oh, when should we turn in Zeus?" Marco frowned. "Probably best to do it right away, don't you think? Get it over with?"

"How long before the new puppies would be ready to start training?" Giana asked.

"Oh." Marco thought about it. "So, they'll be born in, say, a month. Can't really test them until they're three months old, at the youngest. Take them to the water park, see how they react to the obstacles."

"Then can we keep Zeus until then? Four months?" Kimo blurted.

Giana turned to him. "So the puppies will be born in late October. Then November, December, January, right, Uncle Marco? You won't be able to take them to the water park until we're into February."

"Yes, but . . ." Marco gave Kimo a long, searching look. "Don't you think that will just make it worse? Why wait?"

"But you don't know that any of the new ones will work out. What if you do your test and every single one of them flunks?" Giana objected.

Marco considered this. "Honestly, there's so much work that goes into training for water rescue, I can't see doing that with Zeus and then sending him to live with another family. If the new puppies can't handle the water park, we'll just have to find others. I've rescued from the mainland before—there are water parks in California. I can go on a day trip, test out some puppies, bring one back." Marco smiled sadly at me. "I know how tough this is, because I'm going through the same thing with Bear. There's just a difference between work-ing dogs and pet dogs."

"But why send Zeus to the rescue?" Giana demanded. "Aren't they crowded as it is?"

"That's true."

"And there's no reason *not* to keep Zeus until the Newfies are ready," Giana argued. "Bear could use the company."

Marco gave her a grin. "Like mother, like daughter. When your mom was your age, this is how it went. She'd just keep arguing until I gave in. Okay, you think about it, son. But if it were up to me, I'd get it over with."

"Thanks, Dad," Kimo muttered. He was staring at the ground, even though there weren't any balls or treats or anything interesting there.

"Good." Marco said. "We have a plan."

Kimo nodded miserably. When Marco went back in-side, my boy knelt and put his arms around me. "Not the plan," he whispered.

Giana, nearby, seemed to be thinking hard.

The next several mornings, Kimo abandoned me and I was forced to lie around with Bear. It was that school thing again. When he finally returned home, we did Work.

One such day, Giana rode over on her bicycle and Bear and I were put on leashes, and then we took a long walk, not up into the hills but down the street, turning corners until eventually we arrived at the most won-

derful place ever. I smelled it long before we arrived—
the scent of canine was so heavy on the air, I nearly
swooned. Soon we were near a wide fenced-in area with
several dogs running around inside. Even Bear seemed
excited.

I scratched at the gate when Kimo led Bear and me
to it. He opened it, unsnapped our leashes, and let us
run.

Bear jogged in his usual boring fashion, but I took off
in a big wide circle. Several dogs my age immediately
noticed. They ran at me as a pack, looking like this was
their park and they wanted me to know it.

I held my ground, and at the last moment they broke
off, looking at the ground and sniffing pointedly at a
tree, ignoring me.

All but one dog, that is. He never slowed. He came
at me so fast and hard I had no time to react before he
barreled right into me, knocking me off my feet.

I instantly recognized his scent. This was *Troy*, my
brother dog! Giana and Kimo had miraculously led me
to my favorite littermate. We immediately began wrestling in the dirt. I let him pin me and then I pinned him.

"Wow, these dogs look like twins!" Kimo exclaimed.

A girl around Kimo's age approached. She smiled
shyly. "Hi," she greeted them. "My name's Brooklyn."

"I'm Kimo," Kimo responded, grinning. "This is my
cousin, Giana."

"Troy's my dog. Well, he belongs to my family. And

I know your dog. It's Zeus, right? He's Troy's brother. We were there when your father adopted Zeus. I mean, I *think* it was your father. From, like, the rescue patrol or something?"

"That's him!" Giana agreed.

"We're going to do some work with Zeus now. Do you want to watch?" Kimo invited.

Troy and I had stopped wrestling for the moment and settled into good behavior, two dogs sitting and watching our humans, who had the tantalizing scent of treats in their pockets. Since no hands were reaching for those treats, we decided the time had come to go back to being dogs. I jumped on Troy and he responded by fake snarling, pulling his lips back, and giving me a harmless growl before flopping over on his side.

"Okay," Kimo announced. He pulled out a sock, which he rubbed on his hands. "Now, let's see what Zeus can do."

I heard him saying my name, but frankly, Troy was being very distracting.

"Can I help?" the girl asked.

"Sure, Brooklyn," Kimo responded.

I began to think that probably Brooklyn was what they called Troy's person.

"Tell you what. We'll let Zeus smell the sock and then you go hide it over there behind those barrels. He'll be so focused on play, he won't even see you go."

Kimo held the sock out for me to sniff. "Scent, Zeus!"

I smelled it—something smoky and something with a bitter tang. I saw Brooklyn accept the sock from my boy, but then Troy lunged for me and I was forced to jump up on my rear legs and push him back down. He got me on my back and I wriggled in the dirt, and I never even noticed Brooklyn walking away.

Twelve

H^{ey!"} The tone in Kimo's voice brought me instantly alert. I recognized that it was time to do Work. I sprang to my feet.

Troy didn't understand Work. He shoved me with one shoulder and barked when I didn't respond. But I had my eyes on Kimo. This was no time for wrestling, not even with Troy.

"Zeus. Search. Search."

All my attention flowed into my nose, and I instantly found the clear scent of that sock. Yes, I could do this. I began tracking, my nose in the air, moving one way and then the other, steadily advancing away from where Giana and my boy stood. I noticed Brooklyn rejoining them.

I wasn't thinking about other dogs, I was just focused on that sock, homing in on it. I never even saw Troy until suddenly he crashed into my chest, knocking me over.

Didn't Troy understand what we were doing? I tried to focus on Search, sniffing for the sock, but he was there again, digging his snout affectionately into the back of my neck. I turned and shoved him away.

Troy slammed into me again and I stared at him in disbelief. What had happened to my brother? How had he become such a worthless dog? Didn't he know the purpose of life was to do Work for the people who asked? He'd heard them say Search. Surely he understood what I was doing. I resolutely began coursing back and forth, with Troy harassing me the whole way.

Bear wasn't any fun, but at least he knew better than to interfere with Search. At the moment, he was peeing on the base of a tree a short distance away, calmly letting me get on with my Work. Troy should follow his example.

I made ever-widening sweeps, my nose alternating between ground and air. Troy bounced around me, bowing to invite me to play, wagging his tail hard, but I ignored him. At one point, when his muzzle was right in my face, I had to give him an irritated growl. He stared at me in shock, but what did he expect? We were doing Search.

Then I had the scent. Just like that, I'd found it. There were some steel barrels containing delicious-smelling garbage over to one side, but fighting its way to the surface of those pungent odors was the clear signal that the sock with Kimo's scent was lying in wait. I zeroed in on it.

ART #7 TK

I found the sock and, as I had been taught, I did Sit and Speak, barking to let my boy know I had succeeded. Troy joyously joined his voice to mine, but his bark wasn't one of discovery or of signal. His bark was the bark of a dog who didn't know why he was barking but felt sure it was appropriate. It was a little crazy-making.

I smelled rather than heard Kimo and Brooklyn approaching around the barrels. "Good dog," my boy told me.

There were no words I loved more. He had a chicken treat for me and we played pull-on-the-sock, Troy shoving his goofy face into the middle of the game.

We did Search a few more times in that dog park. Always, Troy tried to distract me. Always, I managed to ignore him. Even though the sock was placed in more and more challenging positions (at one point it was actually *in* the metal can, with the garbage), I always managed to find it. I always signaled with a bark and Kimo always told me, "Good dog." He'd give me a treat. (He also gave Troy a treat, for some unknown reason.)

"Your dog is so well trained," Brooklyn said with admiration in her voice. "How'd you do that?"

Kimo shrugged modestly, "Well, my dad's a dog trainer. Zeus is learning to be a water rescue dog."

"Oh," Brooklyn replied, looking impressed. "I didn't know they had water rescue here."

Kimo shook his head. "We don't. I think we should."

He exchanged pointed glances with Giana. "But apparently, there's no money in the budget, so we're raising Zeus and then, when he's fully trained, my dad's going to sell him."

Kimo swallowed hard. I glanced at him, curious at the sudden change in his emotions.

Brooklyn's eyes were wide. "I couldn't stand it if we got rid of Troy. He's my best friend."

"I know," Kimo replied quietly.

We left shortly after that.

"She was cute. Brooklyn," Giana remarked, as we walked up the sidewalk.

"Stop, Giana."

When we arrived home, Bear trudged over to his usual spot and collapsed with a groan. Tutu Nani came out of the house and approached Giana and Kimo. "He hasn't been eating normally," Tutu Nani told them. She bent down to stroke Bear's head. "Do you think he's sick?"

Kimo called to him and Bear grudgingly climbed to his feet, but he was somber and didn't react much when I sniffed his face. Kimo bent down and peered into his eyes. "Are you okay, Bear? Okay?"

I wondered if Kimo could smell the sadness coming off Bear as clearly as I could. It was the sadness of a dog who has no Work to do.

Several nights later, Giana and Auntie Adriana Mom

came over for a meal that filled the house with succulent odors all day. "Happy Thanksgiving!" everyone said joyously. After a while, I figured out that this meant "Dogs get even more treats than usual!"

"I'm going to take Bear to the vet tomorrow afternoon," Marco remarked that night. "Something's not right." He regarded Kimo. "Please stick around tomorrow. I've got some roofing shingles coming at one o'clock. They'll drop them off in the driveway. I need you to move half of them around to the backyard, stack them every two feet."

"Two feet? Should I measure?" Kimo asked, his voice innocent.

Marco smiled. "Okay. *Approximately* every two feet. They're heavy, but don't go getting all muscly on me."

Kimo grinned.

Marco chewed and swallowed a delicious-smelling mouthful. "The Newfie had her pups yesterday. Three boys, one girl," he said after he swallowed.

Kimo glanced away.

I tried to cheer up Bear early the next morning, gnawing a squeaky toy right in front of him, but he just sighed and looked away. He perked up, though, when Marco's Jeep pulled in the driveway. "Come on, Bear. Let's go to the vet." Marco looked at Kimo. "Don't forget about the shingles."

"Okay, Dad."

"I'll make sure he doesn't forget," Tutu Nani promised.

Marco and Bear left, but Kimo stayed. No school. No day camp.

We were playing with the ball-in-a-sock when Tutu Nani joined us in the backyard. She wore a frown on her face—an unusual expression.

"There's a man here who wants to see your dad," she told Kimo. "Says it's urgent."

Kimo frowned, too. "If it's an emergency, he should call nine-one-one."

"I don't think that's exactly what's happening."

"Oh. Okay. I'll talk to him," Kimo offered.

I followed my boy and Tutu Nani to the front door, where a man stood on the steps. He smelled dusty and was coated with a marvelous animal odor. I sniffed his legs carefully.

"Afternoon," he greeted, his craggy face split in a smile.

"Aloha," Kimo replied.

"Name's Diggs. Diggs Riley."

Kimo reached out and grabbed his hand. "Kimo Ricci."

"Your grandma says your dad's not here?"

"Right. He took his dog to the vet." Kimo glanced at Tutu Nani, then back at the man. "Can I help?"

The man's wrinkled face was kind. He gazed at Kimo with pale eyes. "Well, it's my dog, Blue. He's come up missin'. I thought maybe your dad's tracking dog could find him. I stopped by the Search and Rescue and they said they don't do lost dogs and gave me your address."

"That would be Bear, but he went with my dad."

"What about that one?"

Kimo glanced down at me, and I met his gaze. "Um, I've been training him." He stood up a little straighter. "Zeus can cover an area in ten minutes that would take a couple of humans three or four hours. Only, I have to be here for a delivery at one o'clock, so I can't go until after that."

"Oh," Tutu Nani put in, "you go ahead. I'll be here to make sure the shingles get delivered, and you can stack them up when you get back. Your father has holiday shift today, so he'll be late. You'll have time before he gets home."

"Zeus ever looked for a dog before?" the man asked.

Kimo gave a nervous laugh. "Actually, Mr. Riley, he's never really done anything but train before. I understand if you'd rather not take the chance."

"Call me Diggs," the man offered. "And I'll do anything to find my dog."

The man drove a Jeep, just like Marco. Kimo strapped down my crate in the back of it, and I eagerly jumped in without being asked. Wherever we were going, I was sure it was going to be wonderful fun.

We bounced and rode for a long time, much longer than any ride I had ever taken before.

"So Blue really ain't much to look at, " the man told

Kimo, "but he means the world to me. He's a cattle dog, so he works, but honestly, he's more like a member of my family."

Kimo nodded. "I completely understand what that's like."

When we finally got to wherever it was we were going, the smell that had clung to the man's clothing (I was starting to think of him as Diggs, since that was what Kimo kept calling him) was powerful on the air. Something somewhere nearby was causing these odors. It was definitely animal.

Diggs stepped out of the Jeep. "Alrighty, then. So how do we do this?"

"Okay," Kimo responded. "Have you got some things, like maybe some dog toys? We'll let Zeus smell them and he'll catch the scent and then we'll tell him to go look for your dog."

"Simple enough." He was a nice man, and when he bent down to smile at me, I could feel his warm regard for dogs. "I sure hope you can find my big Blue," he murmured. I wagged.

Before long, Diggs produced a couple of squeaky toys. I could tell by the way Kimo held them to me that I was supposed to learn the smell, before he even said, "Scent." Were we about to do Search Work? I gazed up eagerly at my boy.

"I think he's got it," Kimo announced happily.

"Great!" Diggs clapped his hands together and a small cloud of dust flew up from them. "Let's saddle up and we'll head on out."

Kimo froze, so I did too. Something was happening. "Saddle . . . up?" he repeated slowly.

"Yes, right," Diggs responded jovially.

"So, maybe I should tell you I've never ridden a horse before," Kimo advised nervously.

"Nothing to it. You probably surf, right? This is easier than that, I guarantee it. Come on over. I'll put you up on Kelby. She's a real gentle lady. You'll be fine."

As we approached a fence, the animal smells separated so that a very distinct odor wafted toward me on the wind. My nose told me there were some creatures directly in front of me, but I couldn't see anything. Then there was a loud snort from above and I nearly fell down as I scrambled backward. There *were* animals, almost right on top of me, so tall I hadn't really seen them. I stared in alarm and amazement, and they eyed me back with long, expressionless faces.

Diggs led Kimo over to one of these creatures as I anxiously watched. With some fumbling, I saw my boy *climb up on this beast's back*. I was astounded. What was he doing? What was I supposed to do? Bite it?

"Okay," Kimo announced. "I guess I'm ready."

"Look, with horses all you have to do is let them know you're in charge, all right?" Diggs instructed. "Hang on tightly to the reins, don't let them try any funny business. If she doesn't go the way you want, you pull her head the way you *do* want, understand?"

Kimo bit his lip. "Sure."

Diggs easily got onto his own huge creature, and now, to my astonishment, the two giant animals begin plodding along, one next to the other. "Come on, Zeus," Kimo called over his shoulder.

Nothing like this had ever happened before. I followed the two lumbering beasts, noticing that my boy held leashes in his hand. He was taking the monsters for a walk!

"All right, Kimo." Diggs chuckled. "Maybe you're leaning a little bit too far to the left."

"Sorry," Kimo stammered.

"I'm just sayin', ya look like you're about to fall over. Straighten yourself up, son."

Kimo held himself stiffly upright. "Okay," he agreed.

"Pretty sure we should start lookin' where most of my herd has gathered, near the watering hole, edge of my property."

I anxiously glanced up at Kimo. I wanted us all to go back to the Jeep!

The thick scents of the giant walking creatures were soon doing battle with another, new kind of animal smell. Up ahead I saw a different sort of monstrous creature, many of them, some lying down. We kept heading in their direction and I faltered, falling behind. I did not want to engage with a whole pack of giants.

The new animals all turned to look at me as I reluctantly approached, and I could feel the fur climbing up on the back of my neck.

I would not let them hurt my boy.

Thirteen

Some of the animals had their long noses stuck into clumps of grass. Some were standing and staring at me and chewing. I couldn't be sure which posture was more of a threat, so when I barked, it was at all of them, letting them know about the danger that they all faced. I was a *dog*.

They had a very odd way of revealing their terror. In fact, they didn't seem to react at all, even though I was being very threatening. I'd seen that in other animals: a completely paralyzed fear.

"Zeus! Cut it out," Kimo called down to me. I could tell from his sharp tones that he was backing me up as we faced this enemy.

"'S okay. First time a dog sees a cow, can be a bit intimidatin'," Diggs said with a chuckle. "Don't worry, though, they ain't gonna do anything to Zeus. They're used to dogs."

"All right, Zeus," Kimo called to me. He leaned over but didn't climb to the ground. In his hand, he held a long rope toy that smelled like the same dog I had sniffed on the other toys. "Scent."

Immediately I forgot all about the huge creatures and I looked up alertly. This was Work!

"Zeus, Search!"

All right, I needed to find the dog whose scent was painted on the rope. I ran back and forth, seeking the odor that I held in my nose.

There. I alerted. The dog scent was faint on the ground.

"Good dog, Zeus."

"What's it mean?" Diggs asked.

"Zeus has the scent but he's not sure what direction go just yet."

"Well, we're pretty close to the end of my property. My fence line's just ahead." Diggs shook his head. "This is how I knew something's wrong. I can't think of any reason why Blue would leave the herd." He gave Kimo a bleak look. "You suppose someone stole him?" Diggs nodded at Kimo's surprised expression. "He's a valuable ranch dog. Smart, too—my granddaughter's even taught him how to surf."

"I hope that's not it."

"I just . . . I just want my dog to be okay," Diggs choked out in a rough voice. He wiped his eyes.

"Zeus, Search!"

I dashed ahead, still looking, and found the scent

again, stronger and more reliable. I tracked it steadily and then came to a halt. The scent was painted against some wood. There was a fence here, but it was broken, its pieces lying in the dirt.

"Well, look at that." Diggs whistled. He and Kimo approached on their ridiculous, slow-moving creatures. "That must have just happened recently. I ride this fence line couple times a week." He easily slid off his monster.

"Do I need to get down?" Kimo asked nervously.

Diggs smiled. "No, you can stay up there. Hang on."

Diggs dropped to his hands and knees, peering at the soil. I walked over and licked his face. "Yep." He stood back up. "The tracks tell me I got a calf who went this way, and an adult, probably the mom, right on its heels." He pointed through the fence. "Got ourselves a little jailbreak here. That's why Blue's gone, though I can't tell ya why he didn't just steer mother and calf back to the herd." He slung himself back atop the big creature.

Kimo pointed directly at the gap in the fence. "Zeus, Search."

I trotted through that fence hole. The dog's scent was mixed together with that of the strange, huge creatures who had been gathered under the trees. It seemed that the dog and a few of the big creatures were traveling together. I couldn't imagine why any dog would want to do that, but I still had Work to do.

I ran on ahead. When I crested a small ridge, I

looked down and saw the dog I had been tracking, lying patiently next to two of the ridiculous creatures, one smaller than the other.

The dog regarded me cautiously and seemed alert, in case I was some kind of threat. I sat and barked, letting Kimo know with my voice that we'd found what we were looking for. The dog's ears twitched at the sound, but he did not move. He remained lying in the dirt.

"Zeus," I heard Kimo call, so I turned and ran back to my boy. "Zeus found Blue," Kimo explained to Diggs. "I can tell by the way he barked."

"Well, you're a good dog, Zeus," Diggs told me, relief all over his craggy features.

We plodded through the rest of the grasses to the top of the ridge. "Ah," Diggs muttered disgustedly. "Looks like the little one got herself stuck in those logs." He jumped off his giant creature. "Y'all hang back here, please. I'll take care of this."

I watched as Diggs made his way down to the dog and the two strange big creatures. The dog instantly reacted, running forward with his ears down, his tail wagging, a sob in his throat. Diggs was his person, I realized. The dog might keep strange animal company, but he had a person, just like me.

Diggs knelt and took the love from the dog, kissing him and holding him. Then he cautiously approached the two larger creatures. The biggest one raised her head and looked alarmed, but Diggs didn't hesitate. He

ART #8 TK

knelt down again, seized a large log, and pulled it. As soon as he did so, the smaller of the two big creatures jumped free. It ran in a circle like a happy dog.

The dog and I sniffed each other cautiously. He didn't seem particularly glad that I was there.

"Guess I didn't realize how long that was going to take," Kimo remarked, as the big creature under him turned around.

"Woulda taken longer on foot, though," Diggs replied.

Before long, the two dogs, the people, and the strange big animals had covered the ground all the way back to where the lazy animals were gathered under the tree. They still seemed amazed to see me, and I suppose that was only right. I was, after all, a dog, and they were just *big*.

"I can't tell you how grateful I am," Diggs said, as he helped Kimo jump off the giant ridiculous creature. "You two sure are a good team." The man cocked his head, sensing, as I did, that Kimo was suddenly sad. "Why the long face, son?"

Kimo was silent for a moment, probably doing what I was doing, which was breathing in the pungent smell of all the overly large animals. Then he sighed and shrugged. "We're not exactly a team. My dad's got to sell him."

The man frowned. "Whatcha mean?"

"It's what he does, I mean for a living. He trains dogs

for water rescue and then we sell them at an auction in Europe."

I nosed my boy's hand to give him some comfort. Weren't we having the greatest day, doing our Search Work?

"I understand. Bein' a rancher, I gotta sell animals all the time, even if I've developed a real affection for 'em," Diggs replied. "Anyway, just wanna say I'm grateful for your help. You want to come back and ride horses again, you're welcome, any time."

Kimo laughed weakly. "Thanks. I sort of prefer surfing."

In Diggs's Jeep, Kimo kept looking at his wrist.

"You late for something?" Diggs inquired, concerned.

"We had a delivery today at my house. I was sort of supposed to be there. That was a few hours ago. My dad usually gets home around now. He was counting on me."

"You want me to talk to your father?"

Kimo shook his head. "No, it was my decision."

I recognized the smell of our house long before we turned into the driveway. Marco's Jeep was there, and I lifted my leg on it happily. Then we trotted inside.

Tutu Nani smiled at Kimo. "Your dad said to send you up to help him and his friends with the roof. Would you like something to eat, first?"

Kimo nodded his head. "Was he mad about the shingles?"

Tutu Nani waved her hand. "Don't you worry about it. I moved them myself."

"What?"

"They weren't that heavy. Just took a lot of trips, is all." Tutu Nani put a bowl on the table. I smelled fruit but no meat. Kimo didn't mind and attacked it with a spoon.

"Thanks, Tutu."

"Only . . . let's keep this afternoon between us, shall we? I know your father would be unhappy I did that. He thinks I'm an old lady, but I'm not. I'm plenty strong. I'm *healthy*. He finds out I moved the shingles, he'll be after me to go to the *kauka*."

"The . . . kauka?"

"Doctor," she translated.

They talked some more and then I joined Bear in his unhappiness as we lay in the backyard and watched several men walk around on the roof, banging things, lifting things, and throwing things off the roof that were no fun to chase.

Later, the men climbed down and talked and I went to bed with my boy. I thought about the lost dog and the immense creatures he lived with. Though he was surrounded by glorious smells, I knew my life was so much better. He did have a person, but I had my boy, my very special boy.

"What'd the vet say about Bear?" Kimo asked, the next morning.

Marco was chewing toast, which Bear and I found

fascinating. "There's nothing wrong with Bear, physically. Turns out he's just depressed."

Kimo frowned. "How could a dog be depressed?"

"Well, think about it," Marco suggested. "Bear's had a job—an *important* job—working with me every day in search. Then when he couldn't do that anymore, he went with you to day camp, and he decided his job was to help watch children. Now he has no job at all. Dogs need a purpose."

Kimo seemed to be thinking hard. "So what're you going to do?"

Marco smiled. "I have a few ideas. My friends are coming over to help finish the roof this morning, and then I'll spend the afternoon working with Bear. Speaking of day camp, how's it going? Are you able to keep up with your homework?"

Kimo nodded. "Yeah. And we're not just interns anymore. Now we're getting paid for watching the kids."

Tutu Nani brought a plate over and sat down, and Bear and I lifted our noses toward her. Something on her plate was *wonderful*. "School is very important," she lectured gravely. "If this work you're doing ever interferes, I want you to quit. Nothing matters more than your grades."

"Yes, Tutu Nani," Kimo replied.

Tutu Nani let her hand fall, and small pieces of ham bounced on the floor. Bear and I quickly took care of them. I *loved* Tutu Nani.

A few days later we did day camp. Before the children arrived, we did the Work where Giana flailed her
arms and I dragged Kimo out to her and then dragged
them both to shore. Rescue. There were more fun
things to do, in my opinion, but I still loved it because
it was so important to my boy. I had figured out that
Kimo wanted me to swim near Giana but not *too* near
Giana—an odd concept.

"Drowning people are panicking, so Zeus has to
learn to stay far enough away that he doesn't get dragged
down," Kimo explained.

"It's almost like you had the same lifeguard training
I did," Giana mocked, grinning.

"You had the training, but Zeus didn't. I'm saying
this for his benefit," Kimo replied.

"Ah."

After day camp, I was thrilled whenever Giana and
Kimo put their surfboards in the water! We paddled
out and sat, rising and falling in the gentle swells, riding
them in when Kimo decided it was time.

One day there was a thin man waiting for us when we
returned to the beach. He had an easy smile. I wagged
when he petted me. "Hey, guys."

"Aloha, Noa. Welcome back."

"Thanks. I've been meaning to get out to talk to you
two, but I've been playing catch-up since I got back
from the seminar." He beamed down at me. "Is this the
dog that attacked the baby?"

Kimo winced.

"You mean the dog who pulled the toddler upright while Kimo and I were helping other kids?" Giana corrected. "No, that was Bear. This is Zeus."

The man chuckled. "All right, then."

"Bear's a water rescue dog by training. When the wave knocked over a baby, he reacted instinctively," Kimo explained.

The man looked thoughtful. "So when do I get to meet this Bear?"

Fourteen

Tutu Nani and Marco were sitting in chairs in the backyard when Auntie Adriana Mom dropped us off. "Dad!" Kimo called out eagerly. "The head lifeguard wants to see Bear in action. He might go back to having a job after all! At least on weekends."

I nosed Bear, who gave me a friendly sniff. He was . . . different. He still felt tired, but he smelled like the outdoors (and not just the backyard) and Marco. And the sadness scent had completely vanished.

"We're just sitting here admiring the beauty of the roof," Marco replied.

"Wait 'til you see what your father taught Bear to do," Tutu Nani told Kimo with a smile. She had to fight for a moment before she could successfully hoist herself up out of a low chair. When Kimo stepped forward to help, she waved him off. "Your knees will be old some-day, too," she informed him. "Bear? You ready?"

Marco watched with an amused expression as Tutu Nani carried a box out into the yard. She certainly had Bear's attention, even though I could sense there was nothing to eat in there.

Bear trotted by Tutu Nani's side. I could not figure out why he was suddenly so jaunty. Tutu Nani shook the box. "Twenty-six tennis balls!" she announced.

With a heave, she turned the box over and a glorious wealth of balls bounded out into the grass. Naturally, I lunged for them. How I was ever going to carry all of them in my mouth?

"Zeus!" Kimo called sternly. "Sit! Stay!"

I halted. Apparently I was the only one present who knew what to do with so many balls.

Tutu Nani kicked at the balls with her feet, spreading them all over the yard. Bear was focused, also doing Stay. "Bear, you ready? Bear, put them back! Put them back!" she called.

Bear immediately leaped to his feet. I watched in ut-ter befuddlement as he pounced on a ball, picked it up, didn't chew it, and brought it over to the box. He spat it out and turned for another ball. Soon the container was piled with balls and the yard was dismally empty of any dog toys.

"What a great trick!" Kimo admired, thrilled.

"It's his job, now. Whenever he seems bored, I dump out the tennis balls and he rounds them up," Tutu Nani bragged. "See how proud of himself he is? Bear's happy."

"Brilliant!" Giana proclaimed.

The next morning Tutu Nani threw balls all over the yard several times before driving us to day camp. "Put them back!" she'd say. Each time, Bear gathered them all up. It would be far more sensible, in my opinion, to leave them lying out so that they could be played with whenever the mood struck. But nobody seemed to agree with me.

At the beach, before the children arrived, Bear and I took Kimo and Giana out on surfboards. They seemed to have forgotten the right way to surf, though. A wave would come and we'd start moving, but then the humans would fall off the back of the boards. They wanted Bear and me to remain on the boards, though, so that's what we did.

Later, after Bear and I watched the children play, Giana picked up a familiar object: the doll with the jacket on. She took it out into the pond part of the ocean and tossed it facedown into the calm water. "Bear, Rescue! Rescue! *Rescue!*" she called as loudly as she could.

Bear plunged into the ocean. When he reached the floating doll he pulled it out of the water, and Giana and Kimo clapped.

"His hearing's getting really bad," Giana said sadly. "He could barely hear me."

"I can't imagine how I'd feel if I couldn't hear you talk. I'm going to guess . . . happy?"

"Okay, that's the one joke you're allowed per day. Don't go over quota."

I wagged when a man with a familiar scent arrived on foot. "Aloha," he called. He was smiling at both of us and reached down to touch Bear.

"*This* is the vicious baby killer? He looks like a teddy bear."

"That's why his name's Bear," Kimo affirmed.

"He's the most gentle dog in the world," Giana added cheerfully. She carried the doll out into the calm pool and tossed it facedown into the water.

"Zeus, Stay. Bear! Rescue!" Kimo called in an extremely loud voice.

It was hard not to chase Bear as he tore into the water, but I was on Stay. He hauled the floating doll into the air by the jacket and held it there, dripping, until Giana took it from him.

"And that's what the woman was talking about when she told me your dog attacked her child?" Noa demanded. "*That's* what he did?"

Giana nodded. "That's right."

"Huh." Noa looked at Bear a long time, then turned and pointed to me. "Can *he* do that too?"

Giana and Kimo exchanged glances. "With Bear showing him how, Zeus can figure it out in a day," Kimo promised.

"Then I say train Zeus, and bring them both when you come," Noa decided.

"Mahalo, Noa!" Kimo said, beaming.

After that, we had to do school for a while, even though it didn't make anybody happy. Bear chased balls for Tutu Nani several times a day.

The next time we went to day camp, there was a new kind of Work to do: mimicking Bear as he pulled the floating doll out of the water. Kimo would say the same command, "Rescue!," but it meant something different in the pool with the doll than it did when Kimo and Giana flailed their arms and needed to be dragged to shore.

Figuring out these kind of things was a part of doing Work. But either way, helping people or dolls, Rescue meant being a good dog out in the water.

Bear was no longer sad. He was very focused at day camp, staring hard at the children, even though most of the time nobody needed any help. So I was, too, watching very carefully in case there was someone to do Rescue with.

I also learned Gentle, which meant keeping my mouth as soft as possible. Whenever I snatched a piece of meat from Kimo's fingers, I was told, "Gentle," and I wouldn't get the treat until my lips barely whispered across his hands.

When he held his arm under the water with a toy for me to Rescue, I was also reminded to be gentle. Picking up a doll from the water? *Gentle.*

Then there came a day when a wave breached the wall and swept in like a wind, knocking over the children. Bear and I were told, "Rescue!," and we raced for the water. I reached for the jacket of a little girl, and with my mouth ever so gentle, I picked her up out of the surf.

This had just happened when a woman approached. Most grown-ups were smiling and happy when they greeted us and called us good dogs. She was different.

"You! You there!" she yelled angrily.

I set my little girl gently down in the now calm water and glanced over at Bear. He and I both cringed. Something bad was happening.

I anxiously looked to Kimo, who came hurrying over, his attention on the woman and not on his wonderful dog. "Yes, ma'am. How can I help?"

She pointed to Bear and then to me. "Are these your dogs?"

"Well, yes."

The woman drew herself up. "I'm Mayor McClendon. I've received complaints in my office. These dogs are not allowed at this beach. We have little children playing here. We can't let them be in any danger."

"Oh, no, ma'am," Kimo assured her. "There's no danger. In fact, the dogs are here to help *protect* the children."

Giana approached and I wagged, but it was a cautious

wag, because I could sense some anger and frustration pouring off my person's skin.

"What's going on?" Giana asked curiously.

The woman frowned. "I'm explaining to your friend here that no dogs are allowed on this beach."

Giana's eyes flashed darkly. "Actually, that's not true. These are trained lifeguard dogs. They're here to assist us."

The woman shook her head. "No, you don't have permission for that. Dogs are allowed only as far as the edge of the trees up there." She gestured with her chin. "No farther."

Giana opened her mouth, but Kimo reached out a cautionary hand. "Ma'am, I have permission from the head lifeguard—" he started.

The woman raised a palm like she was telling Kimo to do Stay. "Noa Iona works for me. That means you work for me, too. If you do not take your dogs up into the trees and put them on leashes right now, I will fire you." She cut her eyes to Giana. "You too, if I get any lip."

I saw from the expressions on their faces that Giana and Kimo were surprised, and from their scents, I could tell they were angry. Bear picked up on it too, shooting me a worried glance.

"Have I made myself clear?" the woman pressed.

Giana looked down at the ground with a frown.

"Yes, ma'am," Kimo replied stonily.

We finished out that day tied up in the trees. We were also told to do Stay, which I felt wasn't really necessary. We couldn't very well go anywhere when we were on leashes.

Auntie Adriana Mom picked us up and we went home to smell our people eat bananas. Then Bear did Put Them Back on the balls that only he was allowed to play with.

As soon as Marco walked in the front door, Giana and Kimo ran to him. "The mayor kicked us off the beach under threat of prison," Giana announced dramatically.

"She said," Kimo corrected, "that dogs aren't allowed on the sandy part of the beach, because of the little children. She told us the Bear and Zeus are dangerous."

Marco stiffened. "Dangerous?"

"Like they're going to eat the babies," Giana declared hotly. "Like we brought wolves or polar bears or something."

Marco gave them both a long look. Then he sighed. "Well, there's a saying you may have heard: 'You can't fight city hall.' If the mayor says they're not allowed, then I guess they're not allowed."

"But it's not fair," Giana protested.

"The dogs really help us, Dad," Kimo added. "And it gives them both a purpose."

"I understand," Marco replied. "I know how you

feel. But I work for the city, son. This could blow back on me—the mayor's my boss, too. And . . . in January the Newfie puppies will be old enough to take to the water park. Roger has three for me to pick from. Says they're all smart. So, as far as Zeus goes, none of this really matters."

Kimo looked stricken.

Bear and I each went to our people, nuzzling them, and Giana reached a hand out to pet me on the head.

Marco sighed and left the room. He didn't seem happy either. After he'd gone, Kimo looked at Giana.

"We've got to get Zeus perfect at water rescue before January," he said quietly.

Giana nodded. "We will."

Well, life changed again. Now when we went to day camp, we were leashed to the trees. I could tell this made Bear unhappy, and I was not particularly thrilled, either. We were both impatient until the children left, and then we could do Work in the surf with Kimo and Giana.

Bear was happy with Work, as happy as he was picking up balls and putting them in a box. I liked Work, but the thing with the balls would not have given me any joy.

Bear and I were still on Stay in the trees one day when a man in a brightly colored Jeep like Marco's drove into the parking lot. I wagged because I had seen him before—he was Noa. His white smile flashed at us as he approached.

Kimo waved and Giana trotted down to join us. "Aloha, Noa!"

Noa gestured to us. "Aloha! Why're your dogs tied up? How can they help if they're on leashes?"

Giana and Kimo exchanged glances. "Yeah," Kimo agreed, "but the mayor came and ordered us to leave them tied up here."

Noa frowned. "No one told me this." He pulled out his phone. "Tell you what, let's call the mayor right now."

Noa spoke to his phone while Kimo and Giana went back to playing with the children. Bear and I looked at each other, and Bear laid his heavy head down on his front legs with a long sigh. For a moment we'd thought something involving dogs was about to happen, but now we were back to lying in the shade.

The children departed day camp in a slow trickle. When the last of them had left, we did the Work with the floating dolls and the Gentle Rescue. Noa watched, grinning, as Bear and I stood, dripping loyally, the limp dolls hanging from our jaws while Giana took them from us. "Very impressive," he told us.

A noise from the parking lot caused all the people to turn their heads, so Bear and I did too. The angry woman we'd met before jumped out of her car, slammed her door loudly, and came striding purposefully over to us. Giana, biting her lip, moved over to stand with Kimo.

"Hey!" the lady shouted.

Fifteen

The lady still seemed angry. She pointed to Bear and then to me. "What did I tell you? These dogs are not allowed to be here."

"That's just wrong," Giana interjected.

The lady shot her an impatient glance. "You're a child, and you don't understand what's at stake here," she replied. "You need to leave this to the adults."

I could sense the tension, and it was bothering me so much I felt the fur going up on the back of my neck. I did not like this woman, though I did not know why.

"Good afternoon, Mayor," Noa ventured calmly. "Seems like we've gotten off on the wrong foot here. Let's start over."

The woman regarded him coolly. "Your lifeguard interns here don't seem to understand how things work. I have advised them the dogs are not allowed on the beach, and yet"—she pointed—"here they are."

"Yes, ma'am. I told them they had my permission," he explained with a ready smile.

"They do *not* have permission," the woman countered. "Noa, I'll remind you, you work for me."

The man was still smiling, but there was a coldness to his grin. "No, ma'am," he corrected. "I do not work for you. I work for the city council, and I've been told personnel decisions are mine to make as long as I remain within my budget. These dogs cost me exactly zero, so they're staying."

There was a long silence.

"I do not think you want to do battle with me," the woman warned softly.

"Oh," Noa replied with his easy grin, "I don't want to do battle with *anybody*. But this is my beach, my responsibility as head lifeguard. I've seen what the dogs can do, and I'm convinced we're better off with them here than not. If you have any issues with that, we need to take it up with the council."

"All right, then," the woman seethed tightly. "Since I chair the council, I'll make sure this topic is on the agenda for a future meeting."

"Mahalo nui loa," the man drawled sarcastically.

The lady turned her cold gaze on Kimo. "Perhaps Animal Control will be more vigilant about patrolling this beach if they get a call from the mayor's office," she suggested. I didn't like the sound of her voice. She was like a dog about to growl a warning.

Giana opened her mouth, but Noa held up a hand. "Tell you what," he countered smoothly. "Why don't you do that? Call them. I'm going to do so myself, explain my position. The rules on service dogs seem pretty clear—I'm sure my friends at Animal Control know them by heart."

The woman narrowed her eyes. She seemed to want to say more, but then she turned abruptly and stomped away.

I hoped we would not see her again for a long time.

After that day, there was a new variation for both Work and surfing. Giana would say, "Zeus! Rescue!," while Kimo, out in the water, waved his arms and then vanished from view. I'd drag Giana out to where I'd last seen my person and then would dive down after the bubble trail, digging hard because my puffy jacket was trying to pull me to the surface. Kimo would grab my handle and I'd pull him up. That part was easy. My jacket did most of the work, and soon we'd both be bobbing on the top of the water.

Then one day Kimo didn't reach for my handle, but I knew I needed to keep him with me while my jacket pulled us up. I did Gentle Rescue, dragging him to the surface while holding his arm in my jaws.

"He figured it out all by himself!" Kimo whooped, as we broke through to the surface. Giana and Kimo praised me over and over, telling me, "Good dog!"

I loved Work, and being a good dog, and Giana. Most of all I loved Kimo.

Surfing changed, because now Giana would stand on a board behind us as both Bear and I clung to the slippery surface. Bear was in front, and I could smell he was less happy than when he surfed by himself. "Good dogs! You're going to win the contest!" Giana sang at us.

Because it made our people so happy, I knew I'd have to get used to this new arrangement. I was very suspicious, though. I figured Giana was planning to jump off the back and leave two dogs to fend for themselves in the waves.

That's just what she did! Both Bear and I immediately flung ourselves off into the water and let the board travel on by itself. Kimo and Giana, swimming in the water with us, groaned.

But not very long after, we decided that although we didn't like it much, we would remain on the board, since that seemed to be what the people wanted. We did it even when we *started off* with no people riding with us.

It was difficult to keep with it very long—the waves would tip us over at some point. But we were figuring out that surfing meant staying with the board, no matter what. So that's what we worked on.

"These are the most brilliant surfing dogs in the world," Kimo told Giana. "I'm amazed you've taught them to do this!"

"Hey, if I can teach *you* to surf, I can teach anybody," Giana responded.

We sometimes did Work without day camp. We'd go to different beaches and meet different people, and they were all friendly.

I loved doing Work, Search, Rescue, and Surf so much I had dreams about them.

I learned to do Stay patiently on the beach while Giana and Kimo both swam out into the waves. When they started waving their arms and ducking down in the water, Stay was over! I'd leap off the sand and head out to them.

After a while, I learned that it made Kimo happier if I first went to the person farthest out from land. Then I'd circle back for the other one. They'd both grab my harness and I'd swim in and get a chicken treat, though sometimes it was cheese.

I was happy and tired after doing all the Work. At home I would sleep until, of course, food arrived on the table.

One night, after dinner, I was helping by standing and watching for crumbs while Kimo and Giana stood at the sink and splashed water. Then Kimo came to me and knelt down, a serious expression on his face. He stared into my eyes. "Zeus," he said quietly, "I've got some bad news for you."

I felt the seriousness of the moment and put myself into an attentive Sit. "I do this every Christmas," he

ART #9 TK

continued. "I go to Indiana to stay with my mom. It's just a couple of weeks. I swear I'll be right back. Dad says dogs don't really track time, especially in Hawaii, where we only have one season. You don't even know that you've been with us now for nearly eight months. I'll be gone, but then I'll be back, and it will be like I never left."

Whatever was going on, I knew he needed his dog. I remained loyally on his heels, following him around. When he grabbed two bags, one in each hand, I started to worry. This seemed a bit like school, when he left with a bag on his back. But I knew it was more serious than school. Something else was going on and I didn't like it.

I was in a full-on panic by the time my boy walked out the door to throw his bags in Marco's Jeep. Tutu Nani stayed behind, giving both dogs treats, even though Bear wasn't nearly as worried as I was. I gobbled my treats down (turkey!), but I wasn't fooled. My boy had left me.

My world had ended.

Kimo wasn't there when the sun rose in the morning. He wasn't there when Tutu Nani put breakfast on the table, or dinner. He just wasn't there at all, day after day.

When Bear and I went with Giana to day camp, he was as focused as ever. But I watched without much interest as the children splashed and played in the calm water. No waves came over the wall, and when the little humans tottered and fell over, Giana was right there to pick them up. She didn't need us. We had been abandoned.

Bear had Work. He filled Tutu Nani's box of balls in the morning and at night. I had no Work. Plus, I missed my boy so much that I kicked his pillows off onto the floor and slept at the part of the bed where he rested his head, breathing in his scent. When Marco walked Bear at night, I followed sadly behind, and I only lifted my leg when I saw Bear doing the same thing.

I still had the strength to eat dinner, though.

Finally, finally, after forever, I heard the sound of Marco's Jeep coming up the driveway. A smell I recognized wafted toward the house and I ran to the front door. Could it be? Was it possible?

When I saw my boy jump out of the Jeep, I yipped out loud. He ran up the front walk and opened the door and I threw myself into his arms, sobbing and licking his face and legs. He sat down on the floor and held me and laughed.

"You silly dog. You silly, silly dog," he told me.

I hoped he understood that he could never ever leave me behind again.

"Mele Kalikimaka," Tutu Nani told Kimo. She handed him a small package that didn't hold anything to eat inside it.

"That means Zeus has been with us for nine whole months," Kimo marveled. "Zeus!"

I wagged, overjoyed because he was happy and saying my name. Then his shoulders slumped.

Tutu Nani's face grew a little sadder, too.

"You're thinking that it's January, aren't you?" she asked. "Next month, your father will be taking the Newfoundland puppies to the water park, which means Zeus is going to be adopted by a different family."

Kimo nodded miserably. "I don't know how I can do it, say good-bye. Zeus is my best friend in the world. It was hard enough just being separated for Christmas break."

I nosed his hand. Kimo was my boy, and wherever he had just been, it hadn't been good enough to keep him there. He'd come back because he and I belonged together.

Giana was happy to see Kimo as well. We went back to day camp on some days and school on others. We did our Work. Life was back to normal.

One such afternoon, we were in Tutu Nani's truck, back in our crates, everyone enjoying the thick odors of flowers and birds and people on the air.

"I have a question," Giana ventured to Kimo.

Kimo gave her a welcoming look. "Shoot."

"You've taught Zeus search and rescue techniques, and water rescue, too. He's almost as good as Bear. But wouldn't that make Zeus more valuable at auction? If he's already learned the skills . . ." She trailed off.

Tutu Nani looked thoughtful.

Kimo nodded. "Right. I get what you're saying. But right now my dad keeps saying we're going to give Zeus back to the shelter and adopt one of the Newfoundlands instead. Like, in two weeks. He's completely given up on Zeus. So I'm going to prove him wrong. Once he's seen the progress we've made, he'll forget about the new dogs."

Giana gave him a shrewd look. "You're buying time?" she asked. "Time with Zeus?"

Kimo shrugged. "What choice do I have?"

Tutu Nani cleared her throat. "You and your father are reasonable people, but sometimes you focus on your plan—what you think *should* happen—instead of on what's actually happening. I thought your father knew about all the work you've been putting into training Zeus. You're telling me he doesn't know?"

Kimo and Giana both shook their heads. Tutu Nani shook hers, too.

"Every day he's more settled into this plan to start training one of those Newfoundland pups. If you want to show him that Zeus could truly be a water rescue dog, I think you should do it as soon as possible. Do you think Zeus is ready?"

Kimo looked solemn. "I think so."

"Yes," Giana stated. "Zeus is ready. More than ready!"

"Then . . ." Tutu Nani's smile was soft. "Maybe the time has come to let your father know what you've been up to."

It was one of those days when Giana came home with us after day camp. I hoped she'd be staying for dinner—she was more generous with handouts than anybody.

Bear burst out of his crate as soon as Kimo opened it, running to Marco, who was working on smearing black, oily stuff from the Jeep onto his fingers. I understood Bear's energy. Even though Kimo and Tutu Nani and Giana were part of the pack, a dog belongs with his or her own person.

I never felt right when Kimo was out of my sight—school was particularly difficult for me. When Marco was gone, Bear did Work and day camp and chased his balls and dropped them into a box, but his real purpose was to be with Marco.

Marco knelt to greet Bear.

"What're you doing, Dad?" Kimo asked.

"Just some routine maintenance on the Jeep. Never ends," Marco grunted.

There was a long silence. Giana poked Kimo in the shoulder and gave him a significant look, nodding toward Marco. "Hey, so, Dad," Kimo ventured, "I need to talk to you."

Marco wiped his hands on a dirty rag. I hoped he wasn't going to wrap a ball in it—I didn't want that smelly thing in my mouth.

"It's Zeus," Kimo continued.

Marco was watching Kimo warily. "What do you want to tell me?"

"I've . . . I've been training him, like you said you wanted me to, and then not just the basics but other things. Search, and water rescue too," Kimo explained in a rush. He nodded at Giana. "Giana's been helping. And Bear helps. Zeus watches Bear and then it goes easier. And anyway, that's what I've been doing. We've been doing."

Marco turned and set his rag down on the Jeep. A wry smile crept onto his lips. "I know."

Sixteen

I snapped my attention to my boy, who had started in surprise. His eyes widened as he stared at Marco. "You *know*?"

"Well, I guess I should say, I figured. My books on search and rescue and training water rescue dogs are in your room instead of on my shelf. And Zeus is behaving totally differently. He's gone from crazy to calm. His eyes track you the way Bear watches me, waiting for a signal to work. Once a dog gets a taste of having a purpose, it's more exciting than playing with any toy."

"So you're not mad?"

"Of course I'm not mad. I said I was giving up on trying to train Zeus, but I never said *you* should. Sometimes a parent sets up an opportunity for a child and hopes the child is inspired to seize the chance."

"Huh," Kimo said reflectively.

"I try to do the same thing with him," Giana added with a nod. "He usually doesn't get it."

Marco grinned, then gave Kimo a thoughtful look. "So, for you to bring this up now, you must feel like you're ready to show me what Zeus can do."

"Yes, sir."

"Well, then." Marco reached up and lowered the lid on the Jeep. "Let's go."

Tutu Nani joined us. Bear and I circled around to the back of the Jeep, impatient to jump into our crates. "Let's see what you've learned, Zeus," Marco told me enthusiastically. I wagged at the affection in his voice.

Bear and I could soon smell that we were headed to the ocean. We parked on some sand, not at day camp but a new place, with rough waves. We tramped down to the water's edge. Kimo carried his pack, and Tutu Nani held a large, soft bag in which I could smell towels. I was so happy, I was racing in circles around my people, digging my paws into the sand, even though I had no idea what we were doing.

"Sit!" Kimo commanded. He snapped me into my puffy jacket.

Work! That's what we were doing.

Giana swam out into the waves. I figured I knew what she was up to. Sure enough, she waved her arms and ducked her face. Marco called, "Bear, Stay!"

Kimo grabbed my handle. "Zeus, Rescue!"

We threw up a spray as we raced off the shore. I powered through the waters, Kimo kicking a little as he clung by my side. We reached Giana and I swam past her while Kimo dove under and came up behind her, encircling her shoulders with his arms. "Stay calm. I've got you. Easy, now," he advised in a low voice.

"I *am* calm. You're the crazy one," Giana replied.

Kimo snagged my handle and I towed them both back to the shallows.

Marco was beaming. "Excellent!"

I could feel how happy everyone was. I was given a meat treat, and Bear was, too, so even *he* was happy— though he was happier when Giana swam out again and he was given the Work of pulling Marco out for Rescue Giana.

When Bear returned, Tutu Nani reached down and stroked my head, and I wagged, feeling her love. "Let me try," she suggested. "You said Zeus needs to be able to pull in as many as four people." She chuckled. "I have to count as at least two."

Marco and Kimo glanced at each other. "When was the last time you went into the ocean, Tutu?" Marco asked with worry in his voice. "The waves are very big today."

Tutu Nani waved her hand dismissively. "I was born in these waters."

"Your doctor—"

"Is a very nice young woman," Tutu Nani interrupted. "Who is not here at the moment. We've got two lifeguards, a paramedic, and two water rescue dogs. If I'm not safe here, I'm not safe anywhere."

"I'd say Kimo only counts as half a lifeguard," Giana put in.

Marco nodded. "All right, you make a good point. Bear. Zeus. Stay."

I wagged as Tutu Nani ventured out into the surf with Giana. She was much larger than Giana—taller and stronger. I watched her in anticipation. When she began flailing her arms, I tensed, waiting for the command that I knew was coming.

"Rescue!"

Kimo and I hit the water and went straight out to them. Giana was farthest out, so, as I had been taught, I circled her first. Kimo guided Giana to grab my harness, and then we swam straight to Tutu Nani. When Tutu Nani seized my handle, the drag stopped me dead in the water. I was still using my legs to swim, but I wasn't moving!

Forcing all my strength into my legs, I paddled harder and faster. I began panting, determined to do my Work. The waves lifted me up and dropped me down, but the people held on. Soon we tumbled through the white foam and my paws found the sandy bottom. I kept digging, trying to pull us all up out of the reach of the water, until Marco came out into the shallows and told me, "Good dog."

All of the humans were standing, smiling and petting me, and treats were handed out. I was even given a brief game of tug on a ball-in-a-sock!

"Let's do that again," Tutu Nani suggested eagerly. She was panting a little, too.

"Maybe we should let you catch your breath."

She grinned. "This is too much fun. Does Kimo need to come out with Zeus, or can he save me all by myself?"

"No, Kimo has to be there for now," Marco replied. "Zeus is like a motor for the lifeguard. Kimo reserves energy by being towed. It's important to have a trained person with the dog, because a lifeguard knows how to handle someone who's panicking. Though you're right, Tutu Nani. Eventually we'll need to teach Zeus to Rescue without a lifeguard with him."

Tutu Nani looked a little surprised. "But wouldn't that be dangerous for the dog?"

Marco nodded gravely. "Panicked people might very well drown themselves and the dog, but human life is more important. We'll train Zeus to swim up by himself and turn his back and hope the person grabs the handle, in case he ever has to try a rescue all on his own. It's not ideal, but it's our last resort."

"Zeus can already do that," Kimo put in.

Everyone looked at my boy. Marco lifted his eyebrows.

"Giana and I have taught him to dive down and pull

unconscious people to the surface and bring them in," Kimo explained. "Also, he's been swimming out to both of us alone, without a lifeguard."

"He's so strong, that if I grab him like I'm panicking, he can keep afloat," Giana added. "With the vest on, anyway. I mean, yes, a last resort, but he's been doing it."

"Let's try it," Tutu Nani urged, smiling.

Bear and I were hearing "Rescue" a lot, but without the tone that meant we should do something. Our ears kept twitching, but other than that, we just waited.

"Zeus, Stay," Kimo told me.

Tutu Nani turned and waded back into the water, and this time Marco went along with her, and so did Giana. Bear became anxious, watching his person. I focused on waiting for a command. I glanced up at Kimo and he again murmured, "Stay," which really wasn't necessary.

When the people were well out from shore, they began waving their arms. "All right, Zeus," Kimo told me.

I alerted.

"Rescue!"

I lunged forward—and then hesitated, because Kimo wasn't running with me. But when he called, "Rescue!" again, I figured it was just another case of people changing their minds on how things should go, the way some days were school and some were day camp.

Marco was farthest out. I powered to him first and he seized my handle. He was heavier than Kimo, but I was able to drag him through the waves. Next, I paddled to Giana. Finally, I turned and swam to Tutu Nani. She was flailing, her head dipping below water, but she knew how to play, because the moment I brushed up against her, her strong hands grabbed my harness.

I dug in, slowly pulling everybody back to shore.

It was *hard*. I was barely moving. I found myself glad that the waves also seemed to want to go to the beach and were giving me assistance along the way.

"This is such good work," Marco praised me as we swam. "You're doing it perfectly."

"Good dog, Zeus!" Giana added.

I was panting now.

"Are you okay, Tutu Nani?" Marco asked.

"Fine," Tutu Nani responded curtly.

Kimo was standing with his feet in the water. I happily looked forward to being told, "Good dog," and getting another meat treat.

When my paw touched the sand, I felt Giana and Marco release me. Tutu Nani, however, kept her hold on my harness. On her knees, pressing down on me, she struggled to crawl out of the surf.

"Are you feeling all right, Auntie Nani?" Giana asked.

Tutu Nani nodded, but she seemed to have trouble speaking. Marco reached for her and stood her upright and helped her up onto the sand.

For a moment, nobody spoke, and then Tutu Nani

smiled. "Maybe that was a little much for me, but it was a lot of fun."

Next, it was my turn to sit and watch while Bear did work with Marco and Giana. I twitched as Giana waved her arms, but I was on Stay. Sometimes Bear did fun Work while I did Sit, which was also Work but not at all fun.

Dinner that night was one of those times when Auntie Adriana Mom came over and Giana was already there. I sat between Giana and Kimo, which I knew was the absolute best position to be in. Neither of them disappointed, though Auntie Adriana Mom came through for Bear, I noticed, her hand quietly cupping morsels for him to gulp down.

"Kimo," Marco announced, "I need to tell you how proud I am of what you've managed to accomplish with Zeus. He's a full-on water rescue dog."

Kimo was beaming. "Giana was as involved as I was," he told his dad.

"That you just said that? It's just one of the reasons why you're my favorite cousin," Giana informed him with a grin.

"Plus, I'm also your *only* cousin," Kimo pointed out.

"Which is the *main* reason you're my favorite cousin," Giana agreed. "But you also share credit."

"What's next?" Auntie Adriana Mom wanted to know.

"From what I've seen, Zeus really understands everything, so now it's mostly just reinforcement," Marco replied. "A water rescue dog trains pretty much every day, relearning, redoing, practicing."

"Well, and there's the helicopter test," Kimo added.

Marco nodded. "We'll work on preparing Zeus for that this summer."

"You'll be taking the dogs to day camp this summer?" Tutu Nani asked.

"Yes, unless the mayor gets us banned from the ocean," Giana replied. "Did you know she sent some sort of official letter to Noa? He says she's just building a paper trail."

"I don't know how she was ever elected," Tutu Nani complained. "I've never met a single person who likes McLendon."

There was a long silence. Kimo looked up at Marco. "So, Dad, you mean. . . . now that Zeus can do water rescue and everything . . ."

"And is so calm . . ." Giana added.

Marco smiled. "I know what you're going to say. I still want to bring on one of the Newfie pups. But we won't send Zeus back to the shelter. You'll continue to train Zeus and also teach the basics to whichever dog we pick. I'll train Zeus, as well—I've got some ideas on how to ease him into his helicopter skills. Then Zeus will go to auction in August, and a year later, we'll sell the Newfie, but by then we'll have another puppy in training."

Kimo frowned. I felt strange mix of emotions from him—relief, but also sadness.

I inched closer so that I could nose his hand. I was sure he'd feel better if he remembered to drop down a bite of food for such a good dog.

Giana glanced at Kimo. "When do you test the New-foundland puppies?" she asked delicately.

"The park is closed Monday to get decorated for Valentine's Day, so they'll let me take the pups in then," Marco answered.

Later, Kimo and Giana sat in his room and talked. "I don't want another puppy," Kimo declared.

"Would that be so bad, though?" Giana responded. "You can train both dogs easily enough. I'll help."

"No, you heard him." Kimo sighed. "He's not going to give Zeus back to the shelter, but you and Tutu were right—giving Zeus all these new skills just makes him more valuable. At *auction*."

I sat and stared at my boy, concerned about his strong emotions, which were springing off his skin as fear and anger and hurt.

"But you knew that already," Giana reminded him gently. "It's always been about August. So we'll use the whole summer to finish training him in search and rescue, so that he can replace poor old Bear. Isn't that the idea?"

Kimo sighed heavily. "I just don't think it's going to work out, Giana. Tutu Nani's right. My dad gets focused on something, on his plan, *fixated*, and that's all he can see. As far as he's concerned, this is just a *business*," Kimo spat bitterly.

Giana was silent a long time. "We'll think of something," she finally ventured.

Kimo didn't reply.

Seventeen

It was a day of school. Again. I restlessly padded after my boy all morning, noting all the usual signs, but then he did something different. We were in his room and he knelt to look into my eyes.

"Zeus. Today you're going with Dad to the water park. And when you come back . . ." He paused, taking a breath. I watched him in concern. "When you come back, you'll have a new puppy with you, a puppy who will live with us. But that doesn't change the fact that you're my dog. Do you understand, Zeus?"

I felt love and fear boiling off him and lifted my paw.

"Right," he agreed with a chuckle. "Shake on it."

The day went on as usual, with Bear out in the yard collecting his bouncy balls for the box, until Marco called me to leap into my crate in his Jeep. Car ride! I wished Kimo could be there to enjoy it with me.

I recognized the clean, pungent smells in the air long

before we stopped. This was the place where Marco first brought me. The place of the slide.

I was confused when I leaped out onto the warm pavement, and then I was even more confused when a smiling man emerged from his car. It was Roger!

I greeted him happily, but I wondered why he was here. Was everything starting over? Was I going back with Roger now, to live with Troy?

I didn't want that. I wanted to be with Kimo.

"Well, Zeus, you've certainly grown all the way up," Roger told me.

He and Marco stood and talked for a moment, and then Roger reached into his car and opened a crate, and I stared in astonishment as three black puppies were placed on the ground. They charged at me in a full-on assault, leaping up to nip at me.

"Girl's Kaylani, the really big boy's Kia, and the smaller male's Makana," Roger advised.

I was being swarmed. I looked to Marco for an explanation, but he was just smiling. "Perfect. Mahalo, Roger. I'll pick one and swing around your place with the other two."

"My money's on Kaylani. She's the smartest of the bunch."

"See you soon." Marco grinned down at us. "Okay, dogs, are you ready for the river?"

When he ran, calling, "Come!," I followed him and the puppies followed me. There was one female in the

pack, and she was faster than the two males, who were tripping over their big black feet as they tried to keep up.

None of them, though, were as fast as I. I decided, as I ran, that I'd be happy to play with one of them, but three was just too many. I was glad that Marco was giving me an excuse to outpace them. When he reached the familiar flowing water, I gratefully soared off the bank, following him as he splashed and went under water.

"Come on, dogs!" Marco called.

The three puppies stood slightly above us, ducking their heads and sniffing each other in confusion. The gentle current was pushing us along between the banks, which were getting higher the farther along we went.

The puppies tracked us, staying even, but no amount of calling could get them to leap.

"Let's try it again," Marco suggested.

We swam upstream until we could heave ourselves out of the water. The puppies were on me instantly, licking my face and trying to climb on my wet fur. I looked to Marco for how I was supposed to handle them—I was thinking a quick growl might be in order.

Marco yelled, "Come, dogs!," and threw himself back into the river. I was not sure what he was doing— hadn't we just gotten *out* of the water? But Come was Work, so doing it again made a certain sort of sense.

This time the female followed me, and after a few more tries, so did the two males. We got out again and

Marco led us down to where the banks were higher, then higher still. We jumped in, over and over, causing great confusion and fear in the puppies, but eventually they all made the leap.

I knew where we were going next. I could hear the waves crashing in the distance. By now I'd spent so much time at the beach that I was able to follow Marco without hesitation, but the little black dogs seemed cowed by the noise. They eventually paddled out to be with us, but the moment a large swell broke over our heads, all three turned and headed for shore.

Marco and I stayed in the waves, and after a bit the female joined us. She stayed in for just one wave. But the bigger male headed for shore the moment he saw the swell, and the smaller male refused to even consider the pool, even with Marco calling and coaxing.

I wasn't looking forward to the slide, but I followed Marco up the steps as he carried the two males, one under each arm. The smaller puppy immediately began crying, while the bigger one came to me for comfort as we sat together on the small platform high above the ground. Then Marco went back down and brought up the female.

It was time for water in the eyes.

Marco flew down the wet ramp and I followed, turning my head away from the spray. We hit the pool at the bottom and the three puppies stared at us in utter panic.

We spent the rest of the day at the slide, but no matter

how many times I went down it, the three puppies simply wouldn't try it at all.

I wasn't particularly happy with the hosing down when we were back at the Jeep, but I'd learned to endure that sort of thing. The puppies were miserable.

We did go to my first house that day, the one where I had lived with my mother and littermates. But Marco didn't take me out of my crate, so I figured we weren't staying. The puppies were another matter. Marco opened their crate and set all three in the grass.

"How'd it go?" Roger asked.

Marco shook his head. "Just . . . well, you were right. If I were going to take one, it'd be Kaylani, but she really doesn't have what I'm looking for."

"Ah." Roger nodded. "Well, I've got families lined up—who doesn't love a Newfie? So what's the plan, now?"

"I don't know. I was really hoping to bring on another puppy before selling Zeus. I thought it might help Kimo get over saying good-bye."

Roger nodded. "Hard to do. I've cried a few tears saying farewell to some of our rescues, myself. But it's what I do. It's the job."

"It's the job," Marco agreed heavily.

Bear sniffed the chemical odors soaked into my fur with great suspicion when we returned home. But Marco took us for a walk, and after a few long leg lifts,

Bear seemed to accept that I'd gone somewhere with Marco and he hadn't.

Kimo burst through the door later and I greeted him, hoping school was over forever. He looked around, ignoring me, then went to the back door.

Marco came up from behind. "Decided none of them would work out," he explained quietly.

Kimo nodded soberly, but once Marco left the room, he grinned and hugged me, and I felt the love and relief pouring off him.

"I don't want any other dog, Zeus," he whispered into my fur. "I only want you."

And then, for a long time, life was normal, the way I liked it. I began to understand that the days had a pattern: when Kimo slept longer, it meant we were going to be doing Work, then watching children at day camp, then surfing or more Work. When he opened his eyes early and groaned, it meant school.

I don't know why such patterns have to change, but they always do. One day Kimo knelt in front of me, peering into my eyes. He talked, and I felt his love, but I had a sinking feeling inside me.

"It's for spring break, also my birthday," Kimo told me, stroking my fur. "I go every year. It's only a week. You'll be fine." My worries grew worse when I saw him carrying his bags—not the one for school that went on his back but the two heavier ones he carried in his hands.

And then he was gone, out the door and into the Jeep and away from me.

Forever. It was terrible.

And then he was back! Overjoyed, I raced around the yard like a puppy, ignoring Bear's disgusted looks. "You are such a silly dog," Kimo told me fondly. "A silly, silly dog."

Silly dog was like *Good dog*, full of love and approval. I hoped we would never see those two bags with handles again.

We still did school, still did day camp. One day we were at the beach, watching the last of the small children being picked up, when my boy announced, "Tomorrow's Prince Jonah Kūhiō Kalaniana'ole Day."

"What do you want to do? No school, no day camp," Giana replied.

"Maybe snorkeling. Electric Beach?" Kimo suggested, brightening.

"Deal. I wonder how Zeus will react." They both looked at me, so I opened my eyes the best I could, though to be truthful, I was ready for a nice little snooze.

I was up and awake, though, the next morning, when Kimo busied himself assembling things into a pack that he wore on his back. They were not his regular school things, however. Something new was going on.

When we walked out of his bedroom, Tutu Nani looked up with a smile. The delicious smell of eggs filled the air and I trotted to where Bear was already sitting by the table, waiting eagerly.

"Your dad's been out all night." Tutu Nani informed Kimo. "A hiker got lost. They're still looking for him."

"Where?" Kimo asked.

"On Lanai," Tutu answered. "They took the helicopter over this morning. What is it, Kimo? Something's bothering you."

"It's just that Dad was really excited to test Zeus for water rescue, because that's what makes Zeus valuable. At the *auction*. But I've also been training him in Search, which would make him valuable *here*. If I'd known Dad had a rescue, I would have asked him to take Zeus. Then I could show him just what Zeus can really do."

Tutu Nani was quiet for a moment. "You and your father have difficulty speaking about the things that are most important to the two of you. I believe, though, that it's up to you to work it out between yourselves."

"He knows how I feel about my dog."

Tutu Nani nodded gravely. "Yes, he does. And he loves you very much. Think how difficult it must be for him, having to choose."

Kimo seemed to be thinking hard. I nosed him, because it as far as I could tell, the subject of dogs and bacon was not being discussed. "Well, obviously Dad can't drive us to snorkeling," my boy concluded finally. "I'll figure something else out."

Tutu Nani waved her hand. "Nonsense. I can drive you. I'm already going that way."

Kimo frowned. "I thought your doctor said you needed to have limited activity."

"I *am* having limited activity. It's Prince Jonah Kūhiō Kalaniana'ole Day and I'm just going to do what I always do, which is to kayak up the coast with my friends. This is our fortieth anniversary of doing it. Don't worry, we'll go slow."

Kimo frowned. "Well, that sounds like it could be . . ." He trailed off.

Tutu Nani was shaking her head. "I got a little winded, that day on the beach with the dogs. Too much activity. Marco practically kidnapped me to the doctor. The two of them worry too much."

Kimo grinned.

"Besides," Tutu Nani continued, "I'll take Bear with me in the kayak. He'll enjoy it and he'll protect me from anything that could go wrong."

We went for a car ride in Tutu Nani's truck, stopping to pick up Giana along the way. Eventually we hopped out at a parking lot and Tutu Nani drove away. Bear stayed in his crate in the Jeep, but I got to jump out with Giana and my boy.

Humans spend a lot of time going on car rides to parking lots, though to dogs they really aren't all that special.

Something in Kimo's pocket made a noise. He took

out his phone and talked at it while I scanned the ocean, looking for people waving their arms.

"How's your father?" Giana asked, after Kimo put the phone back in his pack.

"Tired," Kimo responded. "They found the guy, the hiker. He's going to be okay, a little dehydrated." He paused. "Dad's not happy about Tutu Nani going kay-aking today. But what was I supposed to do? She's a grown-up."

"You could have duct taped her to a chair."

"Well, sure. He reminded me she's supposed to be getting rest."

"Right, but she's also supposed to be getting exer-cise," Giana argued. "You kind of can't do both at the same time."

"This is why I say you should be a lawyer."

"Why, because my cousin Kimo's always getting into trouble?"

Kimo grinned. "Because you always make a good argument. My dad tells me what to do and I just do it. You come up with reasons why he's wrong, and the next thing I know, he's giving you money."

Giana laughed, so I wagged.

I thought we would probably do Work, or surf, but instead it turned out to be the strangest day yet.

Eighteen

First Kimo put down a blanket. Then he jumped up and down on the sand, holding onto a handle which was connected to a thick stick. The blanket (they kept calling it a "raft") became soft and puffy, like a bed.

Kimo and Giana put on big, floppy shoes and stuck tubes into their mouths, and I rode on the raft like a surfboard while they swam. At one point Kimo raised his head and spat his tube out of his mouth. "Honu! Did you see it?"

"That's Grizzly!" Giana exclaimed. "He's the oldest sea turtle at Electric Beach. He's supposed to be more than a hundred years old!"

"He told you his name?" Kimo hooted.

"This is stuff everyone knows but you," Giana loftily informed him.

I really couldn't relax on the bobbing, shifting raft,

and I was happy when Kimo and Giana finally turned toward shore. "Come, Zeus!" Kimo called, as the waves began crashing in the sharp rocks. I plunged off the raft and into the surf, but he didn't need me to do Rescue. Strong currents of unusually warm water tugged at us, and soon I was up on sand, shaking myself and wagging.

We sat at a rough table and ate food handed out by a nice man in a big truck. Giana and Kimo shared the meal with me, the best dog in the whole parking lot. I was happy.

Later we strolled along the shore, the waves slapping angrily at the beach. Other people were out in the water, waving their long shoes in the air. "I like how few snorkelers there are here. It's a tough spot with all the waves and rocks when you first put in," Kimo remarked.

"I love Electric Beach. The water's so warm from the electric plant, and the fish are so huge!" Giana agreed.

"The turtles are a bit old, though."

Giana laughed. "Okay, that's the one joke for today."

We returned to the shade. "It's weird she's not here yet. She's never late," Kimo said with a troubled glance at his wrist. He picked up his phone and punched at it. "Hi, Tutu Nani," he told his phone. "You told us you'd be here at five and it's pretty close to six o'clock. Give me a call back." Kimo frowned at Giana. "I have a bad feeling about this."

"What do you think's going on?"

"I don't know. My Tutu's the most reliable person in

Hawaii. Something must have happened." They stared at each other. "I'd better call my dad."

Kimo spoke to his phone again. I yawned. There was sand to run in and ocean to swim in and the fabulous smell of food in the air, drifting out from the truck where the nice man fed people. Plus Kimo had his dog right there next to him. With all that, I felt there were far better ways to spend the day than holding a phone to his face. But Kimo often did things that were a mystery to me.

I wagged when he put the phone in his pack. Treat?

Kimo glumly faced Giana. "Tutu's truck's not at the house and my dad say there's no sign of her. Her note says she's going out in the kayak and that she'll pick us up when she's done."

"When she was trying to get out of the water after Zeus rescued her," Giana said a little shakily, "I was so scared. I thought something really bad was happening."

"She said it was nothing. She says my dad worries too much."

"I think we all worry."

Kimo nodded.

"What does your father think we should do?"

"I guess just hope that she's delayed and also lost her phone somehow. Maybe she tipped over and her friends helped her to shore and in the process the phone sank or something. I don't know. He's coming to get us. Maybe by the time we get home she'll be there."

I watched as Kimo bent over the raft and picked at its surface until it began hissing at him. Within moments it collapsed, eventually turning back into a flat blanket. I lay down on it with a groan. Time for a nap?

No. Kimo and Giana were anxious about something, and it made me anxious too. I sat back up, concerned.

When Marco pulled up in his Jeep, I was wagging, but I stopped when I saw the grim set of his face. Had I been a bad dog?

"No sign of her," he announced gravely. "I think she's lost."

We climbed into the Jeep. Kimo closed the door on my crate, and then he put his fingers through the mesh. I licked them because I could sense that my boy was worried.

The Jeep drove along, vibrating in the way that made me want to slide into a nap, but because of the worry I could feel between the people, I was too nervous to sleep right then. Marco turned to Kimo. "I talked to her friends. They said your grandma didn't show up at the place they were all meeting to go kayaking. But when they got back, they noticed her truck was in the parking lot." Marco paused. "I think she took the kayak out to try to catch up to them and ran into some sort of trouble. She's still out there somewhere."

We pulled into the driveway at Giana's house. She stepped out, then leaned back into the Jeep. "At least Bear's with her."

Kimo nodded nervously.

In our own driveway, Marco turned off the car, but nobody jumped out. I raised my nose, sensing that Bear wasn't in the house.

Marco spoke to his phone again, then squinted at the sky. "The Search and Rescue chopper's tied up. They won't be able to get to us for a couple of hours. A missing person is a lower priority than a boating accident." His gave Kimo a sober look. "I don't know what to do."

"Shouldn't we go look for her?"

"We don't have a clue where to start looking. That's why we need the helicopter." Marco sighed and shook his head. They were quiet for a moment.

"Dad."

Marco rubbed his chin, staring off into the distance. "There are so many places where the shore is rocky and dangerous."

"But Dad . . ."

"We've got to find her before nightfall."

"Dad!"

Marco focused on Kimo.

"Zeus can help. It's not just water rescue we've been doing. We've also been working on search."

"Kimo . . ."

"*Please*. Dad, I promise you. Remember how you told the story of the lost swimmers and Bear found them by sitting in the front of the boat and barking when he got the scent? I bet Zeus can do the same thing."

Marco hesitated. "We have to do the right thing here, son. We don't have any time to waste. She could be in real danger."

"Yes, I know! She could *die*. But Zeus can help find her. I swear."

Marco regarded Kimo gravely, then nodded. "All right. Go get some things of your Tutu's."

I followed Kimo at a run into the house and into the bathroom. When he came out, he was carrying a towel covered with the strong odor of the cream Tutu Nani always rubbed into her hands. We dashed to the Jeep and I jumped willingly back into my crate, feeling the urgency pour off my boy. "Hurry!" he urged Marco.

The Jeep jerked and squealed when it hit the street. We drove rapidly. The scent of the ocean grew strong and stronger until we arrived at a place where the water was calm and many boats bobbed up and down. A large rock wall jutting out to sea reminded me of the wall that stopped the waves from knocking children over at day camp.

We bounded down a long wooden sidewalk that stuck out over the water. Marco jumped into a boat and lifted his arms, and Kimo handed me down to him. They had me sit in the front.

The fear and tension in the boat made me pant. "All right. Scent. Zeus, Scent," Kimo told me. He held the towel, and I inhaled the very familiar fragrance of Tutu Nani. I understood I was doing Search for Tutu Nani, but from a boat? That was a very strange way to do Search!

Kimo tossed the cloth on the wooden platform above us, and with a loud growl the boat surged ahead. Marco sat in back, his hand on a loud machine. Kimo was with me.

There was no smell of Tutu Nani, not on the air or on the surface of the water. As we sped along the coast, I stayed alert, searching for the same scent as on that towel. After a time, I couldn't smell the towel anymore. Odors rushed into my nose, of water and salt, of fish and damp earth and seaweed. But not the one scent I was looking for.

"I'm not sure Zeus is ready for this." Marco peered at the sky. "It's going to be dark soon. Why does she have to be so stubborn? She shouldn't have gone out by herself!"

"Zeus *is* ready," Kimo insisted. "If Tutu's up here, Zeus will find her."

I heard my name and glanced at my boy. He and Marco were silent for a while. The wind in my face keep shoving smells into my nose, so many it was baffling. I breathed in deeply and then, *there it was*. Very faint, but up ahead.

I turned and stared at Kimo and his eyes widened. "He's got the scent, Dad!"

Marco slowed the boat. When he did so, smells came at me more slowly and I could separate Tutu Nani from the jumble of odors dancing on the air. Suddenly, I knew we were where she had been, and I barked.

"Yes!" Kimo was thrilled. "Good dog!"

The boat cut sharply toward the shore, which wasn't a beach but a stretch of tall, jagged rocks with towering cliffs behind them. "If she were on the rocks, we'd see her kayak," Marco declared gloomily. "But she can't be here. High tide is coming; she'd be pinned up against the cliffs." He leaned over and peered intently into the darkening waters, searching for something under the surface.

"Zeus has her," Kimo insisted.

The boat went silent. Kimo pointed into the gloom. "Dad, what's that? See? It looks different."

"I don't see anything."

The waves were smashing themselves against the rocks. I saw nothing, but the smell told me what I needed to know. Somehow, Tutu Nani was there, right in front of us.

When the frothing waves drew back from the looming cliffs, there was a gap, a hole in the cliff face. It was from this gap that her scent was pouring.

Couldn't Kimo and Marco smell her? They were distressed and confused, and the boat was drifting away. I barked.

Kimo stared at me. I sat and barked again. Wasn't that the right thing to do?

"Zeus," Kimo commanded. "*Search.*"

ABOUT #111 THK

I plunged into the waters. Waves rebounding off the cliffs swept back into the incoming surf, tossing me, but I stayed focused on my nose. Then there was rock *over my head*, low and dark, a faint light in front of me. I was inside the hole in the cliffs, getting closer and closer to Tutu Nani.

The echoes of the waves were deafening, and the currents held me back and then propelled me forward. A confusing storm of froth and water crashed into my face.

Then, suddenly, the echoes were louder and I could pull my head out of the water. I blinked and caught a glimpse of Tutu Nani sitting on a rocky beach. She brightened when she saw me. "Zeus!"

I climbed out of the ocean, shook, and went to her, wagging. She reached out with a trembling hand. "Such a good dog," she whispered to me.

"Zeus!" Kimo called.

Tutu Nani and I both peered into the gloom. The boat came through the gap, banging against the rock ceiling. Kimo and Marco sprang up from where they'd been crouched down, once it cleared the entrance.

Marco waved something in his hand and a bright light flooded our surroundings. We were in a big stone room with some of the roof missing. The night was above us.

"Tutu Nani!" Kimo cried. He jumped out of the boat, grabbed a rope, and swam to the rocky beach.

"Stay," Tutu Nani commanded me. Well, this was hardly the time for something like that, but I had to do as I was told. Kimo's feet hit bottom and Marco jumped out and they pulled the boat until it was on the rocks next to a kayak.

"Thank God you came," Tutu Nani murmured as Kimo hugged her. "How did you find me?"

"Zeus found you," Kimo replied proudly. "He scented you all the way here."

Tutu Nani smiled at me. "Good dog, Zeus."

Marco came and hugged Tutu Nani. "You had us worried, Tutu," he told her. Then he looked around. "Tutu Nani?"

"Yes?"

"Where's Bear?"

Nineteen

earing Bear's name made me notice that his scent was on the rocks at our feet, but I could smell that he wasn't nearby.

"I told him 'Go home,'" Tutu Nani replied simply. "Isn't that the command?"

"Yes," Marco agreed. "But home from here? I've never trained him to find home from so far away."

"We need to look for him," Kimo declared grimly.

"Let's get the kayak on the boat first," Marco told him with a curt nod.

"It's broken," Tutu Nani advised sadly. "It was *nalu ino*." She was still sitting, and I noticed her breathing was shallow, almost as if she were panting.

Kimo looked puzzled.

"*Nalu ino* means 'rogue wave,'" Marco explained. "You've seen those before."

"Not really," Kimo replied. "Like a tsunami?"

"No." Marco grabbed one end of the kayak and Kimo grabbed the other and they heaved it aboard our boat. "A rogue wave is just a big wave that comes together from several smaller waves. When it hits, it can be massive. A tsunami is a wall of water created by an earthquake. A way bigger disaster."

"Well, the rogue wave was a disaster for this kayak," Kimo observed.

Marco held out an arm and Tutu Nani grabbed it, struggling to her feet. "Bear and I were out in the water," she explained breathlessly. "I was looking for my friends when nalu ino came and capsized the boat and threw us up against the rocks. Bear swam to me and pulled me into this cave. And the waves tossed the kayak in here, too, all broken up. But Bear . . . Bear saved my life, Marco."

"That's what he does," Marco noted quietly. "Do you feel okay, Tutu?"

I was watching Tutu Nani with increasing alarm. Pure distress was pouring off her, a shocking change to her usual odor.

"This has all been a little much," she admitted. Now standing, she was leaning heavily on Marco.

"Tutu!" Kimo exclaimed.

All of a sudden, with a gasp, she sat down.

Marco pointed to Kimo. "Kimo, call an ambulance. Now," he instructed in a firm voice. Kimo dove for the boat and pulled out his phone. I watched him with concern—he was desperately afraid, his hands shaking.

Marco turned to Tutu Nani. "It's okay, Tutu," he murmured gently. His head was close to hers and he had a hand on the side of her neck. "Your pulse is really going. Can you talk?"

Tutu Nani nodded. "Yes," she rasped.

"All right. Are you having chest pains?"

Tutu Nani nodded again.

"Okay. I'm right here," Marco told her, his voice soothing. "Let's just stay calm. Everything's going to be fine. What I want you to do is slow your breathing, okay? Deep, controlled breaths. Try to relax. Can you do that for me?"

Tutu Nani took in a steady, measured breath.

"Dad! No signal!"

Marco gave Kimo a grim look. He turned and studied the gap in the rocks that we'd come through. "One of us needs to get out there, find a signal." He peered up. "Helicopter can't get to us here. We'll need to take her out."

"I can't move," Tutu Nani moaned.

Kimo and Marco stared at each other. "It's going to take us a long time to load her into the boat," Kimo murmured. "You should just *go*. Get a signal. Call for medevac. I'll stay here with Tutu."

Marco bit his lip.

"When we hear the chopper, Zeus will swim out with both of us. We can do this, Dad. Just go!"

With a decisive nod, Marco turned to the boat. He and Kimo shoved it out into the dark water, both of them wading in above their knees. I assumed we would all be climbing in, so I swam out with them, but Tutu Nani was still on shore. I paddled, circling, confused.

"You learned how to do CPR for lifeguard training. You may have to," Marco told Kimo in low tones.

Kimo swallowed and nodded.

Marco gave Kimo a tight smile. "I'll be back as fast as I can."

I watched in confusion as Marco leaped into the boat and headed away without us. Kimo waded ashore and picked up his phone. A narrow beam of light sprang from it, though it didn't smell any different.

Tutu Nani was still sitting on a spit of sand among the rocks, and Kimo crouched next to her, his expression anxious.

"I'm sorry, Kimo," Tutu Nani muttered.

"You're going to be fine, Tutu Nani. There's nothing to be sorry about. Just rest."

On the other side of the gap below the rocks, I heard the familiar whine of the boat's machine starting up.

For a long, strange time, all three of us were both holding still and feeling restless. The tension wafted off Kimo, mingling with the distress and pain from Tutu Nani.

I paced back and forth until Kimo told me Drop and Stay. I tried to be comfortable in the rough, cold sand, pressed up against Tutu Nani's leg. I could feel some of the fear leaving her as I lay there, so I didn't try to change position. Having a dog nearby always makes things better.

This was certainly a strange place. The ceiling hung down low and the light bounced off it and the water. Small pebbles rattled every time a wave sloshed in through the opening where Marco had vanished with the boat. Some of those waves blocked the gap completely with water, but most of them left some room at the top for odors and sounds to wash in.

I heard it before anyone: a familiar thrum beating the air, heavy and loud. I stared expectantly at Kimo.

At first he acted as if he couldn't hear it, and then he jumped up. "That's it! Tutu Nani, the helicopter's coming. Can you get into the water? Do you need me to carry you?"

"I can make it." Tutu Nani crawled toward the water and Kimo followed her and I followed Kimo. I felt the sudden drag as he snared the handle on my jacket. "Rescue!"

This was a different sort of Rescue, and I hesitated, confused. Normally, when we did Rescue, I'd pull the people to shore. But we'd just *left* the shore. Which way was I supposed to go?

I decided Kimo must want me to find Marco and the

boat. I could no longer smell either one, but I gamely dug in. Tutu Nani gripped my harness, too, floating on her back. Kimo swam next to me, working almost as hard as I was.

"Wait. Wait for time between waves," he panted. Then suddenly his voice rose. "Go now Zeus!"

I paddled as hard as I could, and then we were out in the dark ocean.

The thumping noise was very loud over our heads. "Keep going!" Kimo told me. "Let's get away from the cliffs, Zeus!"

I heard my name and I knew he was telling me that we were doing Work together. I followed his lead, swimming straight out into the night.

Now I could see something, harsh fingers of white light playing along the water as the thundering noise in the sky moved slowly toward us.

At the edge of the glow I glimpsed an object bobbing up and down, and I recognized the sound of the boat that had brought us here. Suddenly a beam flashed from the boat and found us. The boat surged ahead.

"Kimo!" Marco shouted above the racket.

"Dad! It's okay, she's okay!"

The noise was overwhelming, thudding into my body, throwing off a stormy wind that threatened to push me under. But I kept swimming. That was my Work, and I knew I had to do it, no matter what.

Marco pulled up in his boat and dove out. I assumed

he wanted me to drag him, too. That was going to be hard Work, but I headed for him, willing to try.

Marco didn't seize my harness, though. Instead, he waved a hand at the sky, at the thing making all the noise.

I blinked when two black shapes hit the water. More people! Was I going to have to drag all of them through the water?

It didn't seem so. They gathered around Tutu Nani, who released her grip on me. Kimo had already let go when Marco dove in.

No one was paying me any attention. I decided to swim in circles, as I'd been taught in Work. Honestly, what I would have preferred was to swim to shore to get away from the horrendous blast of sound. But I knew that swimming away from Kimo wasn't how Work was supposed to go.

When Tutu Nani and a man wearing dark clothing rose up in the air on a rope, I was astounded. She'd never done anything like that before! The other man with the same outfit quickly followed.

And then, at last, the noise started to fade. The brightly lit, thunder-making machine pulled away and zoomed off into the night.

Marco and Kimo gathered hands beneath me and heaved and I was launched, dripping, into the bottom of the boat. They clambered aboard and sat for a moment, probably feeling just as glad as I was that the terrible noise was gone.

Kimo inched over to me and hugged me and I felt the love pouring out of him. "Good dog, Zeus. Good, good, good dog," he whispered.

I wagged. I knew I'd been a very good dog, but I was glad that he knew it too. A treat would have made things even better, but Kimo seemed to have forgotten that.

Finally, Marco moved to sit up front, by the wheel that he liked to hold. The machine in the rear of the boat growled to life. We headed back out into the dark water, lit by the glowing lamps along the edges of our watercraft.

"Will she be okay?" Kimo asked anxiously.

"I don't know, son. I wish I did. But we'll have to just wait and see."

From Kimo I felt fear and frustration and sadness. When we'd reached the shore, gotten out of the boat, and climbed in the Jeep, he asked, "What do we do about Bear?"

Marco sighed. "Let's just get back home. Maybe he'll show up there. If he's not back at first light, we'll go looking."

Nobody talked much on the drive home. Once we were at our house, Kimo called Bear's name very loudly. We all stayed in the driveway, listening. I did not know why he had shouted Bear's name. Bear obviously wasn't here. Anyone could smell that.

Marco sighed. Kimo looked up at him.

"Don't worry, Dad," he said softly. "Bear's really smart. He'll make it."

"There're just so many roads," Marco replied heavily, staring out into the darkness. "When we're working, we have a police escort to stop traffic whenever it's necessary. So he might not really understand just how dangerous cars can be."

I could smell the anxiousness wafting off of Marco's skin. I sat between him and my boy on the front steps, wondering how I could make things better.

We were still sitting there, and I was starting to wonder if a dog who'd done very good Work didn't deserve some dinner soon, when Giana soon arrived on her bicycle. A light on her head swept out in front of her as she pedaled. She jumped off and switched off the light. "How is she?" she asked, as she ran up.

"I'm getting texts. She's still being examined," Marco told her. "They're calling it a non-ST elevation myocardial infarction. No, that's *good* news, Giana. It means the heart attack was mild, with little or no damage. We're lucky."

"How long will she be in the hospital?"

Marco considered this. "Depends. They'll probably want to keep her for a day or two. They have to decide if she's healthy enough for stents—that's where they put little tubes in her arteries to unclog them and keep them open."

"I'll go visit her tomorrow." Giana frowned, looking around. "Where's Bear?"

Marco and Kimo exchanged grim glances. "Tutu Nani told him to go home," Kimo replied. "She washed up in Mermaid Cave."

"Mermaid Cave? I thought that place was a myth!" Giana exclaimed.

"Tell you the truth, I sort of did, too," Marco agreed. "I'd never seen it before." He stood. "I'm going to get some coffee. Won't be able to sleep with my dog out there somewhere."

Marco went into the house. Giana scooted closer to Kimo. "How're *you* doing?"

"Okay, I guess."

"Come on." Giana bit her lip. "I get how important Tutu Nani is to you. Like, the way your dad is sort of like a father to me?"

"She's a big reason why I decided to live here. In Hawaii, I mean, with my dad," Kimo told her.

After I'd done such good Work, why was my boy still this sad? That night, when Kimo fell asleep, I lay up against him in the bed, feeling his restlessness.

Later, I roused myself from the comfortable heat of my sleeping boy and padded out into the dark house. The front door was open and Marco was sitting on the stoop. He turned his head when I approached and put a hand out to touch me.

"Good dog, Zeus," he murmured, a tremor in his voice. "You really know Search, just like my Bear."

Work takes many different forms for a dog. Sometimes

it is to swim hard and pull people along in the water. Sometimes it is to find Giana when she's hiding. Sometimes it is to locate balls that smell deliciously like fish.

And right now my Work was to sit beside Marco and let him know that whatever he was facing in the world, he was facing it with a dog.

I dozed off but opened my eyes when the birds began shrieking loudly to each other that morning had arrived. Marco still sat on the stoop. As the sun was working its way up into the sky, I first smelled, and then heard, and then saw Giana on her bicycle, wheeling up the street and into our driveway. "Did Bear come home?"

Marco shook his head.

Together, the three of us entered the house. Kimo was putting on his shoes. "Hi, Giana," he called.

"Aloha."

"You two have school," Marco stated. "Better get ready for that."

Both Giana and Kimo drew themselves up sharply. I glanced at them curiously.

"No," Kimo replied firmly. "I'm going to help find Bear."

Twenty

Marco and Kimo looked at each other intensely. I have seen two dogs look like then when both of them want a tennis ball and neither one plans to back down.

"And I already told my mom I'm going to the hospital to see Tutu Nani," Giana put in. "She's going to drive me."

After a pause Marco sighed, suddenly weary, and looked away from Kimo. "I haven't got the energy to argue with either one of you." He looked pointedly at Giana. "Especially you."

Giana smiled.

He turned his gaze back to Kimo. "Speaking of moms, I called your mother. She's been talking to your Tutu, and I guess they've decided between the two of them that your mom will stay in Indiana for now. I told her I'd let her know of any change."

"Okay." Kimo nodded.

Marco looked at me. "Think Zeus would be of any use looking for a lost dog?"

"Oh," Kimo replied with a grin, "I *know* he would."

After breakfast I watched curiously as Marco threw some of Bear's dog toys into Bear's crate in the Jeep. That seemed very strange to me. Why didn't he get Bear and put him in the crate instead? What was the point of taking toys for a car ride?

"Where should we start looking?" Kimo asked.

Marco paused, looking thoughtful. "Tutu Nani told him to go home. But we have to think about what *home* really means to a dog. For us, home means a building, a place. To a dog, it means wherever we are, his people. Bear's going to be searching for my scent. That might not necessarily lead him here. Places where I've been, and especially places where we've been together, might be luring him in a different direction."

I jumped into my crate without being asked.

The concern coming off both Kimo and Marco was raw and sharp. I knew that if I weren't in the crate I could put my head in their laps and they would be comforted. A person will always feel better with a dog's head in their lap.

We drove for a long, unhappy car ride, arriving in a place I'd never been before. The trees were lush and tall. The smell of moisture was heavy on the air, and there were many plants. A footpath led up a hill.

"I brought Bear here a lot to train," Marco explained.

"Bear," Kimo called, his hands near his mouth. Then both of them did the same thing. "*Bear!*" they shouted in unison.

I could feel my ears twitch. Obviously Bear wasn't here; there was no smell of him at all. So why were the people yelling his name? It didn't make them feel any better. I nosed Kimo's leg.

"I don't know what I'm going to do if we've lost him," Marco confessed, his voice breaking. Kimo hugged him. I did a dutiful Sit, since that often helps.

"Maybe he's around but just can't hear us," Kimo suggested.

"Maybe."

"Scent," Kimo told me, holding out an old, chewed dog toy of Bear's. I breathed it in. "Search."

Now I understood why we were here. We were doing Search. Search Bear.

We took a long walk up that well-trodden trail. I smelled many people. I smelled some dogs. But the only hints of Bear's scent that I could catch were very faint, from a long time ago. He wasn't here.

After a while, we turned back. I was starting to feel nearly as bad as Kimo. I'd done Search and I hadn't found anyone. Did that mean I was a bad dog?

"Let's head up the Waimea," Kimo suggested.

Marco shook his head. "I think that's pretty far from

where we started. I'd rather try our campsite." We got in the Jeep again and went for another sad car ride.

I would have felt much better if Kimo and Marco weren't so frantic and if Bear had known how to do Search properly and let himself be found. It would have been a wonderful day, packed with long walks, if we just could have been happy about it. Birds filled the air with their songs and mud lured my nose.

At each stop, I did Scent on a dog toy belonging to Bear, and then Search. But Search never turned out right. I began to feel nearly as bad as Kimo and Marco.

When we got out of the car for yet another walk, Kimo brightened. "Giana just texted. Tutu's being sent home."

"That's good news."

"You were right. They want her to get in better shape before they put in stents," Kimo said.

"She's not going to like *that*," Marco declared.

For a moment, they both smelled happier. I looked up, thinking maybe there might be some treats. But it didn't seem to be the right moment for that.

We'd barely began heading up yet another trail when I smelled Bear. He was close by. Had he finally figured out that Search meant I should find him? I picked up my pace.

"I think Zeus has him," Kimo blurted suddenly. "Look how he's alerted."

I ran faster. Marco put his fingers to his lips and blew out a long, shrill whistle. "Search, Zeus!" Kimo called to me from behind.

I was already doing that!

I galloped ahead. My dog friend had come up this trail. He had sniffed at a large can that held some marvelous odors. Then he had trotted off down the hill. I followed the scent, then halted, looking back uncertainly.

My people were so upset. I couldn't very well leave them, even to do Work. I knew Bear was out there somewhere, but a dog's place is with his boy when that boy is sad.

"Why'd he stop? Did he lose the scent?" Marco asked in despair, as they came closer.

Kimo shook his head. "No, Dad. Look at him. He's worried about us. You told me—we can't get emotional about this. We have to be confident that Zeus will find him. Right?"

Marco nodded. "You're right. Thank you, Kimo." He took a deep, steadying breath. "Okay. Zeus, you're a good dog."

I liked hearing that. My ears perked up a little.

"I know you'll find Bear. I know it," Marco told me.

"Search, Zeus!" my boy encouraged me.

Their mood had lightened. It would be all right to leave them now, and I felt confident that Search was the right thing to do. I let my nose guide me, and soon I was far ahead of my people. Behind me, I could hear Marco's loud whistle, but that whistle wasn't for me. That was Bear's whistle. He was calling Bear.

I sensed the moment that the wind took my scent to Bear. I could feel him turn around, the sudden change on the air when he began heading in my direction.

When he burst out of the brush, he was wagging. He was wet and muddy and tired, but the relief pouring off him made me happy. For a moment, we sniffed each other, each of us wagging hard. His exhaustion was something I could almost taste. Bear had been walking for a long, long time.

Then he lifted his nose and I knew he had picked up the scent of Marco. His tiredness vanished and he bolted ahead. I could scarcely keep up with him. His dash up the hill was as energetic as a puppy's.

When we came around a bend in the trail and Marco saw Bear, the two of them ran together and Bear leaped into Marco's arms. Marco sat and held his dog, covering him with kisses, while Kimo knelt next to Marco and joined him in the hug. I pushed my nose in there as well.

"Such good dogs. Such good dogs," Marco murmured.

When we were done hugging, we headed back along the path, the way we'd come, and both dogs were fed dinner, right there at the Jeep! Bear kept pausing as he ate, gazing up at Marco as if to make sure his person was still standing there.

I hoped this meant Bear might abandon some of his meal, but that didn't happen.

Marco cleared his throat. "Kimo, so much has happened that I haven't even said this to you yet, but Zeus swam in the helicopter's wash exactly the way he was supposed to. And you've trained him not just in water rescue but in search and rescue, too. *Fully* trained him. Kimo, I'm so proud of you I almost don't know what to say. After I told you I was giving up on Zeus, you kept working with him. And he's so good, especially for his age, that I'll never bring on another dog without involving you."

Kimo was beaming, all his unhappiness gone. "Well, Giana helped a lot," he told Marco. "So did Bear."

Bear lifted his head, but then went back to eating.

When we returned to the house, Tutu Nani was standing in the doorway. She was holding a stick in her hand, but I instinctively knew from the way she was leaning on it that she was not going to throw it for me. I probably shouldn't chew it, either. It seemed to belong just to her.

Kimo ran to Tutu Nani and put his arms around her. I followed and jumped up from behind, setting my paws on his back while he wrapped Tutu Nani in a long, deep hug.

Tutu Nani patted him on the back. "No need to worry. I'm fine, Kimo."

We were all together at home, as we should be, and

the urgent fear had left the house. That night Giana and Auntie Adriana Mom brought lots of food for us to eat at dinner. Bear and I sat loyally at the dinner table, waiting for a handouts from Kimo and Tutu Nani and Giana and Auntie Adriana Mom, and none of them disappointed.

"Other than cutting out ice cream, what else?" Marco asked Tutu Nani.

She waved her hand, a delicious food smell wafting off it. "The usual things they say. More exercise."

"All right. A good place to start would be maybe taking one of the dogs for a walk after dinner," Marco suggested.

"I'll go too," Kimo volunteered.

"Maybe you stay and do the dishes, Kimo," Marco countered with a chuckle. "In fact, maybe you could do them right now."

Kimo ran some water in the sink and played in it for a while, and then Marco came into the kitchen to join him. "Dad . . ." Kimo began, looking up from the sink.

"Yes?"

"I was wondering . . ."

Kimo let his voice trail off. After a while Marco prompted, "Yes?"

Kimo didn't answer, and I could tell that all of a sudden he was worried again. What could be wrong this time? I looked up to his face, trying to understand.

"You're wondering. Wondering about Zeus?" Marco guessed gently.

Kimo nodded. "He found Bear. He can do search and rescue, just like Bear used to. Dad, don't you think, now that Bear has to retire and stay home with Tutu all day . . ."

Marco sighed. "Kimo, I'm so grateful to Zeus, and to you as well. But especially since none of those Newfie pups worked out, we've just got to sell a dog this year. If we don't, well—we can't afford to live here."

Kimo stared down into the sink full of soapy water, even though there was nothing interesting in there at all.

"I'm sorry, son," Marco said sadly. "I truly am."

I moved closer to Kimo and sat on his feet so he'd know how much I loved him.

Marco left the kitchen, and a little while later, Auntie Adriana Mom and Giana came in. They picked up the dishes that Kimo had been playing with in the sink and rubbed them with cloths.

"I couldn't help hearing," Auntie Adriana Mom said gently to Kimo. "Want me to talk to my brother?"

"No thanks," Kimo answered dully. "It's not like this is some sort of surprise. He's been saying all along that Zeus will be sold in August." He sighed. "I really thought we'd come up with a way to help."

"Help everybody," Auntie Adriana Mom suggested after a pause.

Giana gave her a questioning look. "What does that mean, Mom?"

"You think my brother's happy about any of this?" Auntie Adriana Mom shook her head. "He knows how much Zeus means to you, Kimo. To both of you, actually. But this is how he makes a living. Working as a paramedic barely pays the bills, and he's trying to build up a college fund for you, Kimo. If he has to choose between a dog and his son, he'll choose his son. Every time." She rubbed the dishes a little while in silence. "But it would be better if he didn't have to choose at all. If you're still looking for a way to keep Zeus, it will have to be one that works for you both. Win-win."

"Yeah, well, now we're lose-lose," my boy responded miserably.

Giana looked as if she was thinking hard.

Twenty-One

From that day on, Bear had yet another new job. Once, twice, sometimes more, he would go out the door with Tutu Nani and they would stroll down the street. I could tell from the way they smelled when they got back that they hadn't gone any great distance, but with each passing day, they seemed to progress a little farther. Apparently, Tutu Nani now liked to take dog walks, something she'd never done before.

Most mornings Kimo rose groaning out of bed, said the word *school*, and headed out the door even though he was still tired. I was tired too. I went to lie with Bear, who was content to rest in his spot in the shade after picking up his tennis balls. He didn't want me pressing up against him, though, and kept getting up to move away. I just wanted a soft dog to lie against, but apparently Bear felt his time was better spent alone.

One day, after Kimo returned home and was throwing

a ball for me in the front yard, Giana arrived on her bicycle. She was panting as she jumped down, letting her bicycle fall. "Kimo, Kimo!" she shouted.

Something very exciting must be happening. I grabbed the ball in my mouth and raced up to Giana, ready to share in her joy.

"What's up?"

"I downloaded the application for the dog surfing contest."

"Okay," Kimo answered calmly. "That's not until the end of July, though."

"I know, but you have to get the application in by May thirty-first. Would you just let me tell it?"

"Sure," Kimo agreed with a laugh.

"All right. Do you know there's a prize?"

"Yes. Well, I mean, a trophy."

"No, there's an actual cash prize," Giana insisted. "We never knew about that, but they give you a check along with your trophy."

"Okay."

"So the rules are if the dog stays on the surfboard, then they're eligible for the trophy. *And* the check! Then it's just a question of which dog surfs the best."

"So how much is the check?" Kimo inquired impatiently.

"That's what I'm trying to tell you," Giana complained.

"No, you're not. You said there's a check, but then you started talking about the rules."

"Kimo, if you don't let me tell you, I'm going to get back on my bicycle and leave you here in all your glorious ignorance."

"All right. What is it?"

"It's *fifteen thousand dollars.*"

I felt Kimo start in surprise. "Wow!" he exclaimed. "That's a lot of money."

Giana gazed at him and there was a long, expectant pause.

"What?" Kimo finally demanded.

Giana shook her head. "You're not thinking. How much does your dad get for a dog?"

"He said twelve thousand," Kimo replied slowly. His eyes grew large.

"Right?" Giana replied. "So all we have to do—"

"So if we win," Kimo interrupted, "I can buy Zeus from my dad. He gets his money and I get the dog. Win-win, just like your mom said!"

"Yes," Giana pumped her fist in the air. "Kimo has an independent thought!"

"All right." Kimo was nodding, and excitement was sparking off him. I danced around him so he'd remember that, whatever was happening, throwing a ball would make it even more thrilling. "We just need to make sure that Zeus is the best surfing dog in the world."

"Zeus *and Bear*," Giana reminded him. "That's how we win—with two dogs! As long as both of them stay on the board, we'll beat everybody else."

Kimo gave her a sunny grin. "You're a genius, Giana."

Giana's smile was very satisfied. "I know that."

I was very happy when Kimo came home after doing school a few days later and set his backpack down with a decisive *thump*.

"Another year down," he announced to me. I didn't know what that meant, but I had the sense things were about to change, and sure enough, they did. But they changed in a way I recognized.

Kimo went back to his old habit of going to day camp almost every day. Once again, it was Bear and me watching the water, waiting for a big wave to knock the little children onto their faces.

But Kimo and Giana didn't always spend their time with the little children now. Sometimes they played with slightly bigger ones, swimming with them and talking to them in the water. "Put your face in!" Giana would tell them. "Turn it to the side and breathe. Good!"

"Kick hard!" Kimo would shout.

We did Work in the mornings, but in the afternoons we surfed. I could hardly remember how I didn't like surfing at first. Now I *loved* it. When Bear and I stayed on that board by ourselves, and it sliced through the water without tipping over until the wave ended with a frothy crash, Kimo and Giana would hand us treats and love us and praise us. That's what made all of us the happiest.

"We're going to win!" Giana whooped. "Zeus, you're going to get to stay with Kimo!"

The days when we didn't stand watch at day camp, Bear stayed home to walk with Tutu Nani and sort out the bouncy balls. Marco and Kimo would take me for a ride in the Jeep. It was Work—the same thing, over and over, with little changes from time to time. And I would always wear my puffy jacket with the handle.

We found a place on a beach where a sturdy platform led out high above the water. There were stairs on the platform, leading down to the ocean. Kimo walked me patiently down the stairs to where the water lapped at the bottom step. Then he threw a ball and I jumped off the stairs and into the water. I loved retrieving balls from the water! It was much more fun than just dropping them back in a box the way Bear did.

After a while, I noticed we were stopping on steps that were higher, and then higher still. I jumped off anyway and it all worked out, but each time the fall was farther and farther.

A few times I tried to show Kimo that it would be much easier if I just ran down to the bottom step, right to where the water was. But if I did that, Kimo didn't throw the ball.

I did not understand this part at all. Apparently, he would only throw the ball if I sailed off the higher steps.

It made no sense. But people don't always make sense. Dogs love them anyway.

"Good dog, Zeus!" Kimo shouted, whenever I jumped. We were playing with a ball in the ocean and I was a good dog. What a wonderful thing.

Eventually, Kimo had me stand on the platform itself. He called my name, "Zeus!," and threw the ball.

Except he didn't. I was fooled and jumped off the platform anyway, falling a long way before plunging below the surface. I came up confused, hunting for that ball. But it was still in Kimo's hand. Unfair!

But then Kimo cranked his arm back and tossed the ball for me, so I forgave him and brought it back, running all the way up the steps to lay it down at his feet.

Marco was there beside my boy. "Zeus learns faster than any dog I've ever seen," he announced with a smile.

That was the new game. I'd just jump off the platform, and as soon as I hit the water, I heard and felt the splash as that ball landed near me. I'd surface, grab it, and head up the steps to my boy.

A few days later, back on the platform, Kimo teased me. "Ready? Zeus, you ready?"

I danced around his feet. I was so excited! But I didn't know why, until suddenly Kimo was running. "Come on, Zeus!"

Chasing! I love chasing! I raced after Kimo, right on his heels, and when he soared off the platform I went into the air with him. We both sank and then surfaced in a froth of bubbles. Kimo grabbed my handle. "Go In!" he commanded. He didn't say that very much anymore; I understood what to do without being told. I pulled him to the sandy shore.

We did that Work for a while. I learned he did not want me to jump off the platform the moment he made his leap. Instead, he wanted me to wait until he was in the water. When he started waving his arm and ducking his head beneath the surface, I knew he needed me, even though he wasn't yelling my name. I gathered the edge of that platform under my paws and thrust.

When I bobbed up to the surface, Kimo had his face down under water. I swam to him and he grabbed the harness and I pulled him to shore.

"He can jump off a three-meter board!" Kimo declared happily, when we were all settled in the Jeep.

"That he can," Marco agreed.

Kimo bit his lip. When he spoke, his voice was subdued. "Is he ready for the helicopter test?"

Marco glanced over at Kimo. "I'd say Zeus is almost ready for the helicopter. It costs a lot of money to hire one. I need to do everything I can to try him out, first."

"What if he fails?" Kimo asked. "Like Bear?"

Marco gazed at Kimo for a long time. "I don't think he'll fail." He reached down and started the Jeep. Kimo didn't say anything.

After several days of day camp and Giana and surfing, we returned to the platform, and this time Giana came with us. When we pulled up in the Jeep, there were some people waiting for us on the sand. They sat aside shiny machines.

Marco knew these men and women, and they lightly punched first Kimo's fist, then Giana's. They greeted me by name, so I knew they were good people.

"Your motorcycles are beautiful," Giana told them admiringly.

"I'd love to have one someday," Kimo added.

"Never going to happen," Marco replied. Everyone laughed and I wagged.

Then Marco declared, "Okay, let's do this."

The people on the machines stood up on them and, with a grinding sound, filled the air with an overwhelming blast of machine noise. It was so loud I felt it in my chest, a thunderous roar. They were grinning as the roar became louder and louder. Kimo, his footfalls completely obliterated by all the racket, walked to the end of the platform and jumped off.

I wasn't sure what to do. There had never been this much noise before.

I trotted to the end of the platform and stared down at Kimo. He was already waving his arm and sinking! My boy needed me!

Without thinking, I leaped off that platform and landed right by him. While I was under water, I could still feel the huge roar in my chest. I struggled against my jacket and took my boy's arm in a Gentle Rescue. When I popped up, my boy remained limp, so I pulled him to shore.

"Those've got to be the loudest motorcycles in the world," Marco yelled to his friends, as we climbed onto the beach.

"Well, it keeps us safe. People hear us coming!" a man shouted back over the noise.

Kimo and I went back to playing, while the blast from the machines kept going. I learned to ignore it and concentrate on pulling Kimo, and then Kimo and Giana, back to the sandy shore.

Finally the people left. It was hard to believe, but they made even *more* commotion as they blasted out of the parking lot than they had made on the sand. I could still hear them a long time after they'd departed.

Marco knelt down and gave me a delicious beef treat. "Are you ready, Zeus? I think you are. You're ready for the helicopter test."

"Dad." Kimo and Giana glanced at each other. "There's something we want to talk to you about."

Marco stood up. "Sounds serious."

"We've entered Bear and Zeus in the dog surfing contest at the end of the month," Kimo began.

"There's a cash prize for first place," Giana added eagerly. "If we win, we get fifteen thousand dollars."

Marco raised his eyebrows. "I had no idea. That's a

lot of money." Then his eyes narrowed. "I think I see where this is going. No, Kimo."

My boy was distressed. I licked his leg. "But—"

Marco was shaking his head. "We're training Zeus to save lives, son. That's important. I know you love Zeus. We all do. But one of these days someone will be drowning and Zeus will be there to save them."

"You said you needed to sell Zeus for the money," Giana reminded Marco.

He nodded. "That's true, but—"

"And you said you get twelve thousand," Giana pressed. "This is *fifteen* thousand, so you'll have money left over for food and vet bills. And Kimo and I will be doing actual lifeguarding soon, which makes a lot more. We can pay for expenses."

"Still . . ."

"Plus," Giana went on, not letting Marco finish, "Bear retired from Search and Rescue because of his hearing, and because he needs to help Tutu get more exercise. But now you have Zeus. He can do what Bear does. He can go out with you to find lost people. He can still *save lives* even if you don't sell him! In fact, he's already done that, with Auntie Nani. Maybe someday he can even show new dogs how to do water rescue, the way Bear showed Zeus."

I was uneasy. Giana didn't sound angry, exactly, but her voice was loud and firm.

"Dad, please? If we get the money, can we buy Zeus?" Kimo implored.

Marco was silent for a long, tense moment. Then he glanced at Giana. "You ever lose an argument?"

Everyone smiled, and I relaxed.

"Not very often," Giana admitted.

"All right. You make a good case. Yes, if you have the money, I'll sell you Zeus."

This time, when Kimo and Giana and I ran off the end of the platform, Marco jumped, too. I was glad the noisy machines had departed, and happy to pull all three of my people back to land.

Twenty-Two

The next day was a day camp day. Kimo and Giana played with the older children in the waves, while Bear and I were on Stay and watching for waves to knock over the smaller ones. A girl I'd met before, Brooklyn, the one who smelled like my brother Troy, and a new boy named Davis, walked back and forth at the water's edge, watching the wobbly kids in the shallows.

"Don't you think Brooklyn's cute?" Giana pressed Kimo, when they came back to tell us what good dogs we'd been.

"Please stop saying that."

We surfed and surfed, before and after day camp. I loved it, though Bear seemed less excited about it. He saved all his enthusiasm for greeting Marco, who sometimes came to pick us up. Other times, Marco sent Auntie Adriana Mom in his place.

One day the man named Noa came to visit Bear and me. Giana and Kimo joined us.

"Aloha, Noa."

"Hey kids." Noa grinned. "Having a good summer?"

"Can't believe it's August next week," Kimo replied.

"Yeah. Time flies." Noa glanced out at the ocean, then back at Giana and Kimo. "You coming to the surfing contest this weekend?"

"We're *in* it," Kimo told him.

"Well, not *us*," Giana corrected him. "Bear and Zeus are in the dog contest part."

"Ah, great. So, Monday, there's going to be a city council meeting. I'd very much appreciate it if you'd attend."

"Us?" Kimo stared at him.

Noa nodded. "You and your dogs. Mayor McLendon's going to try to ban them from the beach. I want the council to see how well behaved they are, so it's not just an abstract idea when I pitch them that I want them for water rescue."

"Sure, Noa. We can be there," Kimo agreed.

"My mom'll drive us," Giana added.

We surfed together, that afternoon and the next. As I had done with Work, I'd learned to watch Bear when we were on the board. If he seemed to be moving to one side, I'd make a tiny adjustment the same way and the board would slice the waves instead of running from them. This made Giana and Kimo very excited.

"They haven't fallen off in *days*," Kimo enthused. He sounded very happy about something.

"They stay on for a couple runs tomorrow, we're sure to win!" Giana replied.

The next morning was a complete break from routine. Bear still did his ball patrol for Tutu Nani, but then she climbed in Auntie Adriana Mom's car with us and we drove to a completely different beach!

Many children and adults and dogs thronged along the water's edge. I was excited to encounter Troy, who was there with Brooklyn and Davis, and surprised to smell the dog who liked to hang out with huge creatures.

"Hello, Blue!" Kimo sang out.

The dog's name was Blue. He sniffed politely under my tail, but he didn't seem interested in playing—not at all like Troy, who was racing around, kicking up sand and water, shaking toys in his teeth.

"Hey there, Kimo," said a man I'd met before. His face was dark and wrinkly and his eyes crinkled when he smiled at me.

"Aloha, Diggs. This is my cousin, Giana."

"Aloha. You two here for the dog surfing contest, I take it?"

"Yes, sir."

"Well then." Diggs turned and surveyed the water. "That's my granddaughter Anna out there on the sailboard. She taught Blue to surf. My grandson Mack's going to take him out. Hey, Mack!"

A boy a little older than Kimo trotted up, smiling. He smelled a lot like Diggs. "Mack, this's Kimo—told ya about that search dog, Zeus, remember? He belongs to Kimo. And that's Kimo's cousin, Giana."

"Zeus, Sit," Kimo commanded. I did Sit, and so did Bear, though he hadn't been invited.

"Hi, Zeus!" The new boy reached out and patted my head. "Thanks for finding Blue for us."

Giana and the new boy smiled at each other.

"They're going to be competing in the dog surfing contest," Diggs told the new boy.

"Okay!" He gave an easy grin. "Have to warn you, Blue took third place last year."

"We may have a surprise or two ourselves," Giana replied.

They left, taking the dog Blue with them.

Kimo turned to Giana. "He was cute. Mack."

"Just stop."

A loud voice boomed, *"Aloha! We'll now begin the sixth annual Oahu Dog Surfing Contest!"*

"All right. This is it." Kimo smiled down at me. "You dogs ready to surf?"

There were so many people and dogs and surfboards out in the water, I was actually glad to be doing Drop and Stay on our board as it lay on the sand. It gave me something to concentrate on. I watched in absolute bafflement as people, standing up on boards and holding huge sails, went flying past us. They would pop over the crest of a wave and spin and then smack back down hard before moving swiftly on.

It wasn't long before Kimo released me from Stay and we ran out into the water, Kimo carrying the board with us. Soon he, Giana, Bear, our board, and I were all bobbing in the water.

But it wasn't just us. There were other boards and other people and other dogs in the water with us! Giana and Kimo were tense and excited, and Bear yawned anxiously. Something seemed different about this particular surfing day.

Bear and I got up onto our board. All around us, other dogs did the same. Big waves swept in. People paddled and pushed and then their dogs would be out ahead of the swells. Most of them fell off, which is not the right way to do surfing. But it never seemed to be our turn.

As we floated in the water, Bear jerked his head up and I caught the scent that had his attention. Flowing from the beach, where the people were densely packed together, was Marco's smell. He was here.

I figured Bear would jump off and go see him. I saw Bear thinking about it, even as Giana called, "Surf!," and the board surged underfoot and Bear and I sliced through the water.

In the end, Bear decided to remain on the board, maybe because it was taking us toward Marco faster than he could have swum. But with his attention on the beach, Bear didn't seem to care as much about his balance. He inched forward and the board wobbled. I dug my claws in hard and shifted my weight, and then the wave splashed over us. That meant we could jump off. Surfing was done!

Marco waded out to us, grinning. "Good dogs! That was amazing! You surfed together!" He didn't know about treats after doing surfing, but I forgave him. He got the excited part just right.

Kimo and Giana soon joined us, panting and smiling. "There were only four other dogs who stayed on their boards," Giana bragged. "And *none* of the other teams have two dogs."

"All we have to do is do one more wave. We're going to *win!*" Kimo added excitedly.

Marco nodded. "I hope so. I really do. Good luck!"

"Mahalo!"

The voice boomed again. "*Second round will be Monsie, Bear and Zeus, Bailey, and last year's third place winner, Blue!*"

We went back out. This time there were far fewer dogs. One of them was Blue, I realized. None of them was Troy.

We clambered onto our board and bobbed. This was part of surfing—waiting for the moment when Kimo and Giana would decide it was time to go.

I glanced over at Blue, who was staring intently at the shore. He reminded me a lot of Bear. His person must be on the beach somewhere, just like Marco was.

"Here comes a big one!" Kimo cried.

"It's huge! Is it a rogue?" Giana asked, worry in her voice.

"I don't know, but this is it!" Kimo replied excitedly.

I felt fear and elation boiling off Kimo as the back of the board lifted and Bear and I shot ahead. We rose up and up and *up* above the surface of the water. I lost sight of the other dogs and concentrated on my companion, who was crouched for stability. We'd never moved this fast!

Ahead of us, the boards with sails were darting in different directions. A girl somewhat older than Kimo flew up into the air and landed with a *smack* on the other side of a wave, grinning as she carved a turn.

Then a boy on another sailing board came hurtling over the same wave. His board slanted so that the tip of it was high in the air, and it crashed down right on the girl's head. Then they were tumbling into the water, their sails collapsing over them.

Without thinking, Bear and I left the board together, plunging into the water. It was no longer time to do surfing. It was time for Work.

A huge wave crashed over us, tumbling us, and we rose, sputtering, looking around. The boy was at the surface, clutching his face and moaning. Bear's powerful shoulders came out of the water as he dug through the current.

Where was the girl? I couldn't see her, but I could

PART THREE

smell her, and I was coming right up on the spot where she'd gone under. She was below me now, and I thrust my face into the water and kicked, struggling against my jacket. My eyes stayed open even though I could only see blurry shapes through the water. I followed the scent down to a drifting shadow.

I reached her and she didn't respond, so I did a Gentle Rescue, my mouth closing on her arm at the shoulder. I raised my head, and now my jacket helped me. Together we rose toward the sun.

She was still slack when I burst through the surface. I could smell Giana, right there, helping Bear with the boy.

"Zeus!"

It was Kimo. He swam up to us, reaching out to cradle the girl's head. He seized the handle on my harness and I turned toward shore without being told. The girl coughed some water, blinking and frowning. "My head," she muttered.

"You're fine. We're towing you in. Okay? Just relax," Kimo told her calmly as we swam. "What's your name?"

"Anna."

"Okay, Anna."

"What happened?"

"A windsurfer hit you in the head and knocked you out for a second. My dog Zeus dove down and brought you to the surface."

"Wow. Is anybody else hurt?"

"Maybe, but you're the only one who got knocked out."

I fought the water as it tried to push us back from the shore, and as soon as my legs found purchase in the sand, Diggs and Marco were right there. "Anna!" Diggs cried.

"Don't touch her!" Marco warned. "Keep her stable." He thrust a short surfboard under the water and Kimo reached out to help maneuver it beneath the girl's head. "Try not to move your head or neck at all, okay?" Marco said to the girl.

"Her name's Anna," Kimo informed Marco.

"Anna, I'm a paramedic. We need to make sure you don't have a spinal injury. Kimo, help me lift the board up on the sand."

Everyone was grim, so I didn't wag when Noa approached at a run, carrying a big box. He knelt down and popped it open.

"Cervical collar, please," Marco told him. "Did someone call an ambulance?"

"On its way," Noa replied.

The boy Bear had done Rescue with came over, holding his hand to his nose. "I'm really sorry," he mumbled.

Marco was fitting a large pillow around the girl's neck.

"Let me see your nose," Noa suggested.

Bear was doing Sit, so I did too.

"Well, it's broken, that's for sure," Noa told the boy, not unkindly. "Are you hurt anywhere else?"

"No, just my nose. I didn't see you, Anna. I'm really sorry."

Anna waved a weak hand.

"Like you to not move, if you can help it, Anna," Marco requested gently.

I looked up to Kimo, who was gazing unhappily at Giana.

"Zeus saved her," Giana told him quietly. "Saved her life. It was . . . it was worth being disqualified."

I didn't understand why some people came and put the hurt girl on a long board, which they slid into the back of a loud truck. Nobody I had done Rescue with had ever wanted to lie on a board afterward, or leave in a truck, either.

Diggs got into the truck with Anna. Blue was instantly distressed. The boy we had met earlier, Mack, came to put a leash on him and tried to calm him down.

"Well, so, congratulations about Blue," Kimo told Mack. "First place."

"Yeah it was . . . Well, mahalo. Sorry how it went."

There was a real sense of weary fatigue as we left. I thought Bear and I had done Work very well, but the people seemed unhappy anyway, and there were no treats.

Tutu Nani drove Kimo and me, while Giana went with Auntie Adriana Mom. Bear rode in Marco's Jeep.

"Zeus saved that girl, Kimo," Tutu Nani told him proudly.

"I know. I get that it was the right thing to do. But we were so *close* to winning the contest." Kimo sighed. "And all that money."

They were quiet for a moment. I was tired, but I stayed alert because they were saying my name, and because my boy was sad. How anyone could be sad after a day of surfing and Work, I didn't know, but humans are much more complicated than dogs.

"When's the helicopter test?" Tutu Nani finally asked softly.

"Tomorrow."

"Do you think he'll pass?"

Kimo nodded glumly. "I know he will. Dad says he's the best dog he's ever trained."

"Best dog *you've* ever trained, Kimo. *You* trained Zeus."

"So when he passes, that's it. August is just two days away. We send Zeus off to auction in August."

Tutu Nani's expression was warm with sympathy.

That night, for some reason, Kimo clutched me to his chest the way he used to when I was a puppy. I tried to lick the unhappiness from his face, but I was unsuccessful.

Twenty-Three

I was excited to take a Jeep ride the next day, especially because the smells were different. Wherever we were going, it was a new place! But Kimo didn't understand what a wonderful day it was going to be. His mood was still somber.

"You've never ridden in a helicopter before, have you?" Marco asked Kimo.

"No."

"Didn't think so. It'll be fun."

Kimo gazed at Marco and shook his head, but he didn't reply.

We jumped out of the Jeep and into something else, a new machine that smelled a bit like a Jeep. Marco put on rubber clothes, which I found fascinating.

Then some men came and said, "Aloha." Two of them were wearing rubber suits as well! They shook Kimo's hand. A woman in normal clothes sat in the front seat and flipped switches, making clicks.

And then the noise started up. At first, it was a whine. Then it got louder and louder, a thumping that shook the world. Kimo's hand curled into my collar. The sound swelled until it was overwhelming, and then I felt that we were moving, like being in the crate in the Jeep.

"First Jim and Gary go in," Marco shouted. "They'll be acting as drowning victims. Then Zeus. Gary will grab Zeus's handle, then they'll swim to Jim. I'll jump in then, assist with the evacuation, put Zeus in the sling for retrieval. The test is to see if Zeus remembers his training in all the chaos."

I was pretty surprised when the two men in rubber suits decided to jump right out of the door of the machine. They probably just couldn't stand the thundering roar any longer.

Marco reached for my harness, but Kimo pulled me away. "Let me do it, Dad."

Marco nodded. He handed a strap to Kimo. "Okay. Fasten this around yourself so you don't fall out."

Something was happening. This felt like Work. I tensed. Kimo made his way over to the open door.

I stared. There was water far below us. And in the water, the two men were waving their arms. I knew what Kimo was going to shout.

"Zeus! Rescue!"

I hesitated. I knew what to do, but we were high up above the water. And the drumming thunder was just so overwhelming.

"Zeus!"

My boy's voice cut through the noise, and I knew what he wanted me to do. Though it was a long way down, I threw myself out the door, plummeting toward the water.

I hit the water feetfirst, and in the next moment my head was under. There was a moment of sweet relief from the pounding noise, but the roar sharpened when I popped my head up.

I swam toward one of the men, circling behind him. He spun and grabbed my handle, which was good. He knew how to do Work.

I turned to make my way to the second man, and I could tell that someone else had jumped out of the machine. I smelled that it was Marco, still in his rubber suit, before he hit the water.

"Rescue!" he called.

He and I met the second man at the same moment, and both of them grabbed onto my harness. Now I was dragging three people. But where was I supposed to take them? There was no shore in sight. There wasn't even a boat. How was I supposed to do Rescue here?

Marco helped. He kicked, pushing us all along, and he guided me toward a wire hanging down from the wildly noisy machine.

"Here we go!" he shouted.

First one man, then the other, both grinning, were fastened to the wire and hoisted quickly up. I saw Kimo watching me from the door of the machine and wondered why he didn't jump down to be with us. It was actually fun to be swimming, aside from all the racket.

"Okay, Zeus. This'll be a new experience for you," Marco told me. I felt him tugging on my jacket. He snapped something into place—it felt like a leash, going into my harness. Then he raised his thumb.

I was absolutely stupefied when my jacket pulled me *out of the water*. I dangled, dripping, looking down in amazement, going up higher and higher as the sound from the machine got louder and louder. Then I felt and smelled Kimo gathering me in.

"Good dog, Zeus," he choked. I licked his face, tasting salt. He was saying "Good dog," but I had never felt him so sad. "You passed the helicopter test."

Marco decided he'd had enough swimming and he too rose up on the cable, swinging into his seat with a broad grin on his face. "Did you see that? We still have training to do, but he never lost his head for a moment. Zeus, you're a true water rescue dog."

"Good dog," Kimo repeated.

I was both exhausted and concerned. Kimo's mood was dark, and he didn't say much as we rode in the loud machine and then in the Jeep on the way back to the house.

"We'll train you in the sling—we've got one at the Rescue—and other than that, you've got the skills, Zeus," Marco told me happily.

I wagged at his approval, but my eyes were on my boy.

The next morning, Marco left the house before breakfast. "Got a hiker fell down into a gully," he explained, as he went out the door. Bear and I were patient watchers under the table, sensing that today might be a bacon day.

We were right!

Giana and Auntie Adriana Mom came over, soon after eating, and we all climbed into Auntie Adriana Mom's car. "How'd it go yesterday?" Giana wanted to know.

"Zeus passed with flying colors," Kimo answered dully.

"Oh. So, so sorry, Kimo," Giana said quietly. She sniffed.

Auntie Adriana Mom sniffed too. Then she drove us to a big building with a cool, echoing interior. I smelled many humans and almost no dogs. My nails clicked loudly. I looked to Bear for an explanation, but he was focused on following Kimo.

I was surprised to find Diggs in the hallway. "There you are!" he boomed. "I saw your name on the agenda and wanted to make sure I spoke to you before the meeting."

"How's Anna doing?" Giana asked.

"Fine. Got quite a lump on her head, but she'll survive, thanks to you." He grinned at Kimo. "Thanks to you, your dog, your dad . . . I'm pretty indebted to your family, Kimo."

"You said you saw my name on the agenda? So you're on the council?" Kimo responded.

"That's right. I guess we'll be talking about dogs today?" He nodded pointedly at Bear and me.

"The mayor wants to ban them from the beach. But Noa—he's head lifeguard—wants them there to help protect the children," Giana explained. "So it's a choice between a mean woman and saving kids."

"Well, that's just crazy," Diggs declared, shaking his head. "I don't understand McLendon. She just seems to enjoy being unpleasant. Should have seen her face when she handed me the check for Blue winning the surfing contest. Mayor McLendon and I don't see eye to eye on much of anything."

"Zeus is being sold, like I told you," Kimo put in. "So it doesn't matter what she says about him, because he won't be around. But Bear will still be at day camp, and if the council allows it, he'd be happy to continue to be a lifeguard dog."

A shadow passed behind Diggs's eyes. "You did tell me that. What's the sale price your dad's asking?"

"It's an auction. He usually gets twelve thousand," Kimo replied sadly.

"I hope you'll vote to keep Bear on duty," Giana told Diggs. "When a wave hits, there's not much time to pull the kids out of the water."

"Oh, you can count on me. I've seen what these dogs can do."

I wagged, because someone I recognized—Noa—came up to us. He was smiling as usual. "Mahalo for coming, guys," he said to us. "'Morning, Diggs."

"Aloha, Noa."

"Well." Noa beamed at us. "Ready to get started?"

I followed the humans through double doors into a big, brightly lit room. People were sitting in rows of seats, watching others sit at a table and talk. "Let's go down front," Noa whispered. "They've finished old business."

I recognized one of the people, a woman, who glanced up at us sharply as we settled down. Diggs sat at a place near her, at the front table. She seemed as angry as the last time I had seen her. Some people just really need a dog, and she seemed to be one of them.

"That's the mayor. She chairs the meeting," Noa explained in low tones.

"We met her," Giana noted dryly. "Not the sort of person you'd want to have lunch with."

"See the woman next to her, the one with the open laptop? Wearing the white hat?" Noa continued. "She's the parliamentarian. That just means she makes sure that all the work is done and recorded legally, according to the rules. Before we had her, the council would decide something at one meeting and then spend the next six meetings arguing over what they had decided."

Giana and Kimo grinned.

"Before we get started," the unhappy woman began with a frown, "I'm going to direct that those animals be removed from the chamber. This is a city council meeting, not a dog show."

Everyone stared at Bear and me. I wagged just the tip of my tail, unsure what was happening.

"Point of order," the man sitting next to Diggs interjected smoothly.

The woman raised her eyebrows. "Yes, Tom?"

"Service dogs are allowed on all government property and in all government buildings. It would be *illegal* to eject them."

The woman shook her head. "I believe that the context of that statute is animals assisting other-abled individuals. These animals, as I understand it, don't do that."

"Well now, hold on there, Mayor," Diggs interrupted. "I'm reading the very rule right here, and it don't say a thing about what *type* of service animals are covered. It just says 'service animals.' And seems like, given what we all know is on your personal agenda today, having these two service dogs in particular would be a good idea."

Annoyance flickered on the woman's face. She brushed impatiently at her dark hair. "Fine. This shouldn't take long. I'll direct your attention, please, to the first item on the agenda, which is a motion by the chair that all dogs, including trained lifeguard dogs, be barred from city beaches." She looked over at us with a cold smile. "Do I have a second?"

"Move to table," Diggs put in promptly.

"I second the motion to table," the man sitting next to Diggs interjected.

There was a silence. "What's happening?" Kimo asked Giana.

"I think 'to table' means they're not going to consider the motion for now," she whispered back.

"Is there a second to the original motion?" the woman persisted in chill tones.

Diggs picked up a piece of paper. "Madam Chairperson, since I got the rules out, I'm reading right in them that the motion to table needs to be voted on first, if there's a second."

"Why would we put this off, Diggs?" she snapped. "You're delaying the inevitable."

"I'm just reading what it says here, ma'am."

The frowning woman looked at the woman in the hat, who nodded her head. "He's correct."

The woman blinked angrily. "All right. All in favor of the motion to table say 'Aye.'"

Two people raised their hands and nodded, while Diggs and the man next to him said loudly, "Aye."

"Against, say 'Nay,'" said the unhappy woman. "Chair says nay."

A woman at the very end of the table meekly murmured, "Nay."

A long silence ensued. "Motion to table carries," the woman in the hat finally noted calmly. "Next time, please say 'Aye' out loud, if you don't mind."

"Sorry," one of the men at the table muttered.

"All right, then. On this very topic, I have a new business motion of my own to make, if you'll indulge, Mayor. I think it will clear things up for you about the dogs," Diggs drawled. "May I have the floor to propose the motion?"

"Clear things up *how*, exactly?" the angry woman challenged.

"Well, if you don't mind, Madam Chairperson, I kinda think that'll all come clear when I say it."

The woman scowled, then nodded curtly.

"Mahalo, Mayor. Now, I don't know if any of you are aware, but we had an incident at the city-sponsored surfing contest yesterday, a collision, and my granddaughter got conked on the head so hard she went under. Nobody saw it happen in all the confusion, except these two dogs, and one of them, the Labrador there, saved her, while the big dog next to him went to assist the boy who collided with Anna. Got a broken nose out of it, which wasn't life-threatening, but my Anna, that's a whole 'nother story. Sank like a stone. Seems that a dog's nose is so good, Zeus here was able to dive down and grab her. These two dogs here are trained in water rescue. My own dog, Blue, now he's good with cattle, and he won the surfing contest, but I wouldn't wanna count on him to pull me out of the drink," Diggs finished with a chuckle.

"I'm certain we all are happy to hear that your granddaughter survived the incident, but you said you had a motion," the woman icily reminded Diggs.

"I'm gettin' there, ma'am. I do like to wander a bit, but I'm gettin' there. So like I said, this dog saved little Anna's life. They could do that for other people, too, if they are on the beach. Our head lifeguard, Noa Iona, has requested that, which in his position he is authorized to do."

The frowning woman opened her mouth but Diggs held up a hand.

"Right, I do understand there may be a bit of controversy over whether Noa has that authority, so here's my motion. We have utilized dogs on the Search and Rescue team all along, but one of them, the big one with the white face, there—his name's Bear—has retired, which sort of leaves an opening. I move that the city authorize Zeus to be on water rescue duty at the sole discretion of Noa Iona, and that we further allow Zeus to be used in Search and Rescue as needed."

My boy sat up straight next to me, staring at all the talking people with rapt attention. I didn't see why, since none of them were eating anything.

"I second the motion," the man sitting next to Diggs said immediately.

Diggs grandly bowed to the frowning woman. "Discussion?"

She shook her head. "Your motion makes no sense, Diggs."

"Well, that doesn't surprise me at all," Diggs replied with a laugh. Several people in the room joined him, and I wagged. Bear looked at me but didn't wag. A dog's life is better if he learns to wag at everything, even if we don't understand what's going on. But that's not something a dog as serious as Bear can understand.

"First," the woman said, the frown still heavy on her face, "you're acting as if we can make whatever decisions we want about these animals. Who actually owns Zeus?"

There was a silence. "I do, Your Honor," Kimo finally replied in a small voice. "Zeus is my dog."

Twenty-Four

The people in the room made small muttering sounds. I wondered if it had to do with the way everyone kept saying my name—my name and Bear's. I glanced at him to see if he understood what was happening, but his return gaze was all Bear—flat and expressionless.

"You don't . . . Please don't call me Your Honor. My title is Madame Chairperson."

"Sorry, Madame Chairperson."

The woman looked around the room, then focused her attention on Noa. "So am I to understand that the dogs who attacked the little girl were under the control of a *boy*?"

"Bear didn't *attack* anybody," Giana objected in a hot murmur.

"Point of information," the man next to Diggs interrupted calmly.

The mayor sighed. "Go ahead."

"If it please the chair, the definition of *attack* is 'to take aggressive action against an enemy with weapons or armed force, to launch an assault, or to take violent action against a person or place,'" the man said, looking down at a paper in his hand.

"For heaven's sake," the angry woman muttered. "Fine."

"To your larger point, Mayor, I've seen this boy in action. He knows his way around dogs," Diggs supplied helpfully.

The woman frowned at Kimo. "How old are you?"

"I'm fourteen."

"Fourteen." The woman gave an exasperated sigh. "All right. Did you know ahead of time that Mr. Riley was going to make this motion?"

"Um, you mean Diggs?" Kimo looked a little panicked, and I edged closer to him. "No, Madame Chairperson."

"How do you feel about it?"

"I guess . . . I'm in favor?"

"So let me get this straight. You're willing to just . . . give ownership of your dog to the city?" the woman asked. "Why would you do that?"

Kimo looked uncomfortable. "Actually, I suppose I can't really do that. He's . . . Zeus is . . . My dad and I trained Zeus to sell. I can't just give him away."

"Oh. Well." The woman turned a triumphant glare

on Diggs. "And would you tell the council how much a trained dog like this would cost?"

Kimo shifted in his seat. I watched him, hating that he was suddenly so unhappy. "Like, my dad says twelve thousand dollars."

"Twelve. *Thousand.* Dollars."

"Yes, um, Madame Chairperson."

The woman raised her hand and frowned at it, holding up her fingers in turn as she said, "Plus food, upkeep, housing, vet bills. Sounds like this little experiment would run the city an awful lot of money. Thousands of dollars, in fact."

"Well, yes, ma'am—I mean Madame Chairperson. But Bear here, he lives with us and always has," Kimo explained. "My dad is on the S&R squad. So we take care of Bear. And there's a fund, donations from people Bear has helped—lost hikers and people like that— which pays for his food and stuff."

Giana spoke up. "Sure seems like the life of a girl who got hit on the head and nearly drowned in a surfing contest run by the *city* would be worth twelve thousand dollars. I mean, imagine what would have happened if the dogs hadn't been there!"

The frowning woman directed a glare at Giana. "Whoever you are, you are not to speak unless the council directs you to."

Giana pressed her lips together tightly.

The woman shook her head, but it didn't do any good—the frown was still there. "I had a feeling you would try to ambush me about something today, Diggs. You were just too pleasant to me in the hallway. Before I came in, I did a quick search about the so-called water rescue dogs. Do you know there are almost no places in this country where these dogs are used? The only references I can find are to Europe."

"She says Europe like it's a *disease*," Giana whispered.

The woman must have heard whatever Giana said, because she directed her scowl toward Giana for a moment.

"At any rate," the woman at the table finally continued, "I don't think our city is the place where this country should initiate a largely untested program. We don't have any facility for the animal, unless it is with the K-9 squad at the police station, or the shelter."

"I'd like to amend my motion, please," Diggs advised cheerfully.

The frowning woman gave him a weary look.

"Further to my motion, I move that Zeus be allowed to continue to live with the Ricci family, and that the Search and Rescue team be allowed to continue to raise donations from grateful *voting* citizens to support vet bills, food, squeaky toys, and the like."

"Second the amendment," said the man next to Diggs, the moment Diggs stopped talking.

The woman shook her head unhappily. "This is a

waste of time. The upkeep of the dog is a secondary consideration. The city doesn't have a spare dollar in the budget, not to mention twelve thousand of them."

Kimo's shoulders slumped. He gave Giana a defeated look.

"You spend more than that every year on fireworks," Giana declared scornfully.

"If I have to remind you again, I will summon the police and have you removed and charged with interfering with a city council meeting. You are to remain silent," the woman commanded.

Giana looked away in disgust.

"All right then, let's move on," the woman said officiously.

"Madame Chairperson, there's a motion on the floor," the woman in the hat protested mildly.

"The motion is irrelevant. There's no money in the budget. We are wasting all of our time on a frivolous debate. I don't appreciate it, Diggs. This isn't the first time you've tried to gum up the works with a load of nonsense."

"Regardless," the woman in the hat objected, "the proper order is to vote the motion up or down. The decision on how to fund it would be a different process."

"We can't fund it!" the angry woman snapped.

"Oh yeah, that's the final thing," Diggs put in smoothly. "I propose, in support of my motions, to purchase Zeus from Marco and Kimo Ricci myself, using my own funds, and donate the dog to the city to be used in the manner I just described. As long as he continues to live right where he is, with Marco and Kimo Ricci."

There was a stunned silence in the room. Diggs winked at Kimo. "Seems like I just came into the money, thanks to some surfing contest."

"Move vote by acclimation," the man next to Diggs said quickly.

"All agreed?" Diggs responded. "Say 'Aye.'"

Everyone at the table except the frowning woman said, "Aye."

"Not in favor? Say 'Nay.'"

Nobody spoke. The frowning woman shook her head. She looked to the woman in the white hat, who nodded. "It was a little irregular, but the motion carried. Mr. Diggs Riley will purchase Zeus, to live with the Ricci family and work in Search and Rescue, and at the direction of the director of lifeguards, Noa Iona, to also work at the beach to provide water rescue services. Implied, therefore, is defeat of the tabled motion to ban dogs from the beach, since they are in direct conflict with one another."

"*Brilliant*," Giana breathed.

The woman gave Diggs a sour look. "Seems like you snuck this one over on me, Diggs."

"Why, Mayor, just trying to help the city out, as always."

She shook her head. "This is ill-conceived. The liability policy on the dog would run us thousands of dollars." Her smile was tight. "As much as your generous offer to help the city is appreciated, Diggs, it appears you didn't think of that."

"Actually, Mayor," Noa corrected, "I talked to my friends at the police and S&R departments. Seems that our umbrella policy covers any dogs employed in public service for any reason. Not that I think these two big guys would ever bite anybody. They're as gentle as lambs."

With a weary sigh, the unhappy woman surveyed all the people in the room. "Very well. This is hardly the first time that the council has embarked on some fool course of action against my wishes. You want these dogs at the beach? Fine. But remember that I warned you this would be trouble." Her frown went even deeper. "We're going to take a fifteen-minute break, and when we return, continue with new business." She abruptly pushed herself away from the table.

I jumped up because Giana and Kimo did. They hugged each other and hugged Auntie Adriana Mom and hugged Noa, and then Diggs came over and they hugged him.

Bear and I glanced at each other. There was just a lot of human hugging going on, but nobody seemed to be thinking of treats for dogs, which was a shame.

We all streamed out into the sunshine. I didn't know what was happening, but everyone was overwhelmingly happy.

"We won!" Giana called out.

"I almost can't believe it. It's amazing," Kimo declared. He turned to Noa. "Did you know about this? What Diggs was planning?"

"He sort of let on in a phone call last night," Noa replied with his usual smile, glancing up at Diggs. "We wanted, though, to make sure we didn't let the mayor know in advance. Lots of ways she could have cut us off at the knees, if she'd heard about it ahead of time."

"She almost did," Giana reflected. "She had some arguments ready."

"Oh, she's a smart woman, no denying that," Noa affirmed. "Not very nice, but pretty sharp. I try to stay on her good side, though honestly it's more like I only get a choice between her bad side and her worse side."

Diggs laughed.

"And thank you, sir," Kimo said. "I never for a moment saw this coming. I was actually thinking about taking Zeus and heading for one of the other islands, live off the land."

Giana's eyes widened. "Are you serious? So you'd be, what, the Dog Boy of Maui?"

Bear and I wagged at the laughter.

"Actually, like I said before, it's me thanking you," Diggs reminded Kimo. "I'da given all my money to get my Blue back, and then Zeus pulled Anna out of the drink. I mean it when I say we coulda lost her in all the confusion. That was a rogue wave for sure, and it threw everyone off their game. I never even knew my granddaughter was drowning. But Zeus knew. Anna means everything to me. Without her, all the money in the world wouldn't make me happy."

Giana gave Kimo yet another joyous hug. "You don't have to say good-bye to Zeus. He gets to live with you, now. He's your dog."

Kimo wiped at his eyes. Then he fell to his knees and grabbed my face in his gentle hands, holding me and gazing into my eyes. I wagged, feeling his complete, un-restrained love. He was happy. Making my boy happy was by far my most important Work—Work that I was glad to do over and over again.

"You live with us now, Zeus," he whispered. "Always and forever. You'll never be sent to live in Europe. You're my dog, and I love you."

Bear could feel all the affection and came over to push his snout into the middle of it. He might have trouble experiencing fun, but every dog knows how to receive love from a person.

I raised my head because I heard the familiar sound of Marco's Jeep. Bear noticed my movement, but he didn't react. When Marco jumped out, his scent reached us, and Bear turned his head, dashing to his person and wagging.

"Hey there," Marco greeted as he walked up. "Sorry I'm late. It took three tries to get that guy out of the gully." He looked between Giana and Kimo. "Did I miss anything important?"

ART #15 TK

Reading Group Guide
Zeus: Water Rescue
By W. Bruce Cameron
Ages 8–12; Grades 3–7

Synopsis

In *Zeus: Water Rescue*, Kimo Ricci's father, Marco, trains and sells water rescue service dogs. But it doesn't feel like "business as usual" when Kimo is instantly smitten with Zeus, an energetic chocolate Labrador puppy Marco brings home for work. Marco cautions Kimo to think of Zeus more as a project than a pet so it won't be so hard for Kimo when it's time to sell Zeus. But spunky Zeus narrates the story of how "his boy" Kimo—with the help of his beloved grandmother, charismatic cousin, and Zeus's newfound best dog buddy, Bear, changes the plan. Despite obstacles and missteps, Kimo and Zeus ultimately find a way to stay together as a boy and his pet dog and do important, literally life-saving work for their community.

Reading *Zeus: Water Rescue* with Your Children

Pre-Reading Discussion Questions

1. In *Zeus: Water Rescue*, Kimo Ricci is devoted to his dog Zeus and Kimo's father, Marco, cherishes his

beloved dog, Bear. Have you ever shared a deep bond with a dog or other pet? How or why was having that particular animal in your life important to you? Or do you have a friend or family member who has had this experience? How would you describe their connection with their special pet?

2. The dogs featured in *Zeus: Water Rescue* are great pets, but they are also working dogs. Have you ever seen a working dog in action or heard or read about one? What job was the dog specially trained to do? How and when were the dog's skills put to the test in a real-life situation?

3. In *Zeus: Water Rescue*, the (human) main character, Kimo, struggles when something he really wants (to keep Zeus permanently) seems to conflict with what is best for his dad's business (training and selling Zeus as a water rescue dog). Kimo has to figure out if and when it is reasonable to challenge the plan his dad has made. Have you ever found yourself in a situation like this with a friend or family member, or can you imagine one? How did you (or how do you think you would) handle this kind of scenario?

Post-Reading Discussion Questions

1. What are your first impressions of Zeus's personality when the pup narrator is first introduced in Chapter 1?

2. Roger, who operates the rescue where Zeus lives at the story's beginning, describes local paramedic, Oahu search and rescue team member, and water rescue dog trainer Marco Ricci as "extremely organized and strategic." Do we see more of those qualities in Marco as the story develops? How do they factor into his work and family life?

3. In Chapter 2, Zeus describes meeting Kimo for the first time: "We looked into each other's eyes, and I could feel it. Every dog has a person. This one was mine." Have you ever felt or made an instant connection like that with a pet?

4. Based on her comments when Kimo returns to Hawaii after visiting his mother, how do you think Tutu Nani (Kimo's grandmother) feels about her daughter's choice to live and work in Indianapolis, far away from her ohana (family) in Hawaii? Do you feel like Kimo's mother is defined more by her absence than her presence in the story? Why?

5. In Chapter 4, Marco tells Kimo: "Zeus will go from being a pet to being a project . . . This'll make it easier for you to accept when we send Zeus to auction." How much does this advice match up (or not) with how the story actually unfolds?

6. In Chapter 5, Kimo confesses to his cousin Giana that he is intentionally training Zeus to respond incorrectly to the "Stay" command. When she overhears this,

what does Tutu Nani tell Kimo about the Hawaiian concept of Pono? Do you think Kimo made the right choice to teach Zeus "Stay" incorrectly? Why or why not?

7. Marco is conflicted at the prospect of separating Kimo and Zeus but wants to be consistent. He tells Tutu Nani: "I have to be consistent with Kimo, be true to my word so that he knows I always mean what I say. It's one of the most important things a parent can do. It's as true for raising children as it is for raising dogs." Do you agree with this? Why or why not?

8. In Chapter 8, Zeus explains: "Work made me feel like I was doing something important and pleasing my boy too. I had a sense of purpose whenever we did Work." Can you think of an example of a home, school, or extracurricular project that gave you a similar sense of accomplishment or purpose?

9. In Chapter 10, how does a joke about Marco never having been the same age as Kimo and Giana turn into a more serious discussion about how the professional path Kimo hopes to follow is similar to his dad's? How does Marco feel about that?

10. In Chapter 12, Zeus is happy to see his brother Troy again but confused when Troy interferes with Zeus's "Work," wondering: "What had happened to my brother? How had he become such a worthless dog? Didn't he know the purpose of life was to do Work for the people who asked?" What do you think Zeus

has learned and experienced to make him feel this way? Include details from the book to support your answer.

11. How do Kimo and Zeus help rancher Diggs Riley with his dog, Blue?

12. Kimo wants to keep Zeus as his pet. What do rancher Diggs Riley, Roger (who operates the animal rescue), and Kimo's dad (who trains service animals) teach him about taking into consideration other important reasons for giving animals away, even if it is difficult?

13. How does Marco's dog, Bear, going deaf and needing to retire from the search and rescue team, play a significant role in the story?

14. In Chapter 18, how do Zeus and Kimo play key roles in rescuing Tutu Nani and Bear after a rogue wave hits her kayak?

15. How and why does Anna's accident during the Ohau Dog Surfing Contest and Blue winning the prize contribute to Kimo's ability to keep Zeus as a pet and give his community access to a vital resource?

16. In Chapter 24, at the city council meeting, how do head lifeguard Noa and rancher Diggs Riley's support for Bear and Zeus as trained and valued water rescue dogs force Mayor McClendon to reverse her plan to ban dogs because she thinks they could endanger rather than protect children at the beach?

17. In *Zeus: Water Rescue*, Kimo learns that it is valuable to consider other people as well as himself when faced with a problem or challenge. How and why do you think this is an important way to view problems and find solutions?

Post-Reading Activities

Take the story from the page to the pavement with these fun and inspiring activities for the dog lovers in your family.

1. In *Zeus: Water Rescue*, canine narrator Zeus forms a deep, loving bond with senior dog Bear. In spite of very different personalities, attitudes, and energy levels, the two dogs use their individual strengths and talents to support each other throughout the story. Zeus often makes candid, funny observations about Bear and how different he is from Zeus himself, as the two dogs live, train, and "work" together. Invite your child to do a drawing, create a cartoon strip, or write an imagined dialogue that highlights the contrast between the two dogs. (They can imagine a situation or select an event from the story to represent in their drawing, cartoon, or dialogue.)

2. Marco Ricci teaches dogs skills and trains them to behave in certain ways depending on unique circumstances. Sometimes Marco harnesses a dog's natural talents and tendencies to make them useful for specific jobs. Marco's son, Kimo, taps into future water rescue dog Zeus's rambunctious nature to intentionally teach him to "Stay" incorrectly, hoping Zeus will fail his water rescue test and get to live with Kimo forever. When this plan takes a turn in the wrong direction, Kimo needs to retrain Zeus to understand and execute the command correctly. With adult permission and supervision as needed, can you try some of the techniques Kimo used to retrain Zeus to help a family dog (or family friend's dog) correct a negative habit or behavior?

Reading *Zeus: Water Rescue* in Your Classroom
These Common Core-aligned writing activities may be used in conjunction with the pre- and post-reading discussion questions above.

1. **Point of View:** *Zeus: Water Rescue* is told from the energetic Labrador pup Zeus's point of view. Zeus's age, enthusiasm, and sense of humor influence his perceptions and descriptions. Zeus lives with and learns from Bear, an older, calmer, and—in Zeus's opinion, though he loves Bear dearly—less fun-loving dog. How might the story be different if it was being told from Bear's perspective? Invite students to explore this by describing a key event from the story in 2–3 paragraphs written from Bear's point of view.

2. **Family Ties:** A lot of the action in *Zeus: Water Rescue* is driven by different relationships within the Ricci family. In a one-page essay focusing on a specific relationship, discuss how family dynamics play a key role in this story. For example, Kimo and his father have a lot of common ground but sometimes lack the communication skills to reach it. Kimo's grandmother, Tutu Nani, tends to offer Kimo insight and perspective rather than black-and-white rules or recommendations. Kimo and his cousin Gianna always have each other's backs despite their mutual sarcasm and teasing. Include details and examples from the text to describe the relationship and explain its significance in the story.

3. **Text Type: Opinion Piece.** In *Zeus: Water Rescue*, Mayor McClendon wants to ban dogs from the beach. She argues that having dogs on the beach poses a potential danger, especially to children, since dogs could bite or attack them. On the other hand, head lifeguard Noa and day camp interns Kimo and Gianna think professionally trained water rescue dogs would help make the beach safer, especially for young children easily knocked over by waves. Write a short essay explaining your opinion on whether you think rescue dogs like Bear and Zeus would be a help or hazard on the beach. Use examples from the text to support your argument.

4. **Text Type: Narrative.** How might *Zeus: Water Rescue* be different if Giana, with her quick wit and sharp debating skills, was the narrator? In the character voice of Giana, write a few paragraphs about a significant event, or events, from the story. Do you think the story would be significantly different if it was told from Giana's point of view? If so, can you explain how and why?

5. **Research and Present: Dogs to the Rescue.** Throughout *Zeus: Water Rescue*, Marco teaches Kimo and Giana how dogs are trained and used for water search and rescue. He also talks about the different characteristics a dog needs to have to be a successful search and rescue or water rescue dog, including the pros and cons of using Newfoundlands instead of Labradors in these important jobs. Invite students to do online or library research to learn more about the Newfoundland or Labrador dog breeds (for example: physical appearance, temperament, and features that might make them good working dogs). Students might also investigate how dogs are trained to be working dogs in search and rescue, water rescue, or other areas. After compiling their research, have students present what they learned in a PowerPoint or other multi-media style presentation.

6. **Research and Present: Hawaiian Handbook.** Zeus: Water Rescue is set in Hawaii. Throughout the

story, we learn about Hawaiian lifestyle, language, and their communities. Invite your students to work in pairs or small groups to research different aspects of Hawaii (for example: language, culture, geography, history, or the different islands). Have the students share their learning in an oral presentation supported by visual and written materials. Students can then work to compile their information and materials into a handbook for Hawaii, which could be put in the school or public library (with permission) for people interested in learning about or visiting the Hawaiian Islands.

Supports English Language Arts Common Core Writing Standards: W.3.1, 3.2, 3.2, 3.7; W.4.1, 4.2, 4.3; W.5.1, 5.2, 5.3, 5.7; W.6.2, 6.3, 6.7; W.7.2, 7.3, 7.7